Antenora

Dori Lumpkin

Creature Publishing
Brooklyn, NY

ISBN 978-1-951971-18-2
LCCN 2024937904

Cover design and spine illustration by Rachel Kelli

CREATUREHORROR.COM
🐦 @creaturelit
📷 @creaturepublishing

To me from ten years ago. Don't worry. You'll make it out.

Antenora

"And in those days shall men seek death, and shall not find it;

and shall desire to die, and death shall flee from them."

Revelation 9:6

I

When I was young, my mother used to tell me that the mountains around Bethel, Alabama were touched by angels. They protected us, she said. The way they jutted up out of the ground, sky-high and endless, keeping us in like a prison. Bethel was in a valley. A perfect valley, she said, keeping us safe from harm and the devil's influence.

Look at how the mountains bend, she would tell me. *How the only thing out here is us and the sky. The devil can't touch Bethel. Bethel is pure.*

I liked to look up at the sky whenever she would tell me this. I'd pretend to be searching for angels, like she said, and that's what I would say if she asked. But I wasn't. I was looking at the gnarled twists in the trees above, searching for faces. I was looking at the curves of the mountaintops, searching for the well-trodden hikers' paths in the Appalachian Mountains, wondering why exactly people sought salvation in these hills. What they thought it would get them. And, of course, I was wondering exactly how easy it would be to get out and join them.

Eventually, she would chide me for not paying attention. She would tell me that I needed a little more of God's grace, a little more patience, a little more obedience.

She'd send me to pray, and I'd be back inside, wondering why it was that angels would move stone to build a mountain to protect just one town. And why that town was even worth protecting in the first place.

She never told me exactly how it was that the barrier was supposed to protect us from the things inside Bethel itself. Or, more specifically, Nora. It seemed a bit of an oversight, trapping people in with a beast and expecting us all to be fine. Putting our souls in the hands of God himself and watching as we all tore each other apart over nothing more than a girl my age.

It didn't start that way, though. Nora wasn't always a beast—if that's what you're choosing to believe about her. She was a little bit odd, don't get me wrong. Always had been. But that didn't matter. She was good. She always had good in her, even if she didn't really understand the way of the Lord.

Nora was my first—and if I'm being honest with you, only—friend.

We met in grade school, back when Bethel was still arguing with the state about whether or not they were allowed to teach us the way they did. Nora liked to argue right back with everyone in Bethel, you see, which is what made her a problem. She was too opinionated. Too brave. She wasn't quiet, didn't keep sweet. She was nothing like the women we were all supposed to learn how to be. I know that Pastor David prayed for her to get bit almost every other Sunday when it was her turn to prove how close she was to the Lord.

The snakes liked Nora, though, which was an obvious sign of the devil to everyone around us. Every time they would get tossed into her tiny hands, it was like she understood them. Their eyes would just glaze over, and the rattling would hush, and she would smile and laugh and say *See? God does love me!*

I didn't like Nora because of the snakes, or because she argued. I didn't even really like her because no one else did (though I do find I have a fondness for the unloved sort of things). I mostly liked her because she felt strong. Strong in the way that trees are strong, like you can hold them and know that they aren't going anywhere, that there are years and years of bark and wood under your hands, and you can trust that. Strong in the way that Pastor David tells us that church is strong. We're supposed to be able to know, without a single question, that Bethel Pentecostal will continue to live on no matter how long it takes all the rest of us to die out.

Nora had her feet planted firmly on the ground, and she rooted herself deep in the minds of every single person in that town.

That's why her possession—if you want to call it that—wasn't really a surprise to anyone at the end of the day. When you've got your feet planted anywhere other than the heart of God, your mind is open for all sorts of influence, right?

Before I continue, I don't want you to think that I'm some sort of Godless heathen. I was raised right. I had gone to Bethel Pentecostal since I was smaller than you can imagine, and my mother and father before me, and then so on all the way back to the beginning of Bethel itself. I had held the snakes, I prayed when Esther Carthage had her cancer, and I was there when it was pronounced that she was saved, even though she wasn't saved for long before death took her. I might be young, but I did my time with my knees pressed against wooden hassocks, knowing that my obedience directly influenced just how much God did or didn't help my hometown. I'm a good girl. I just think that people tend to have a lot of misconceptions about what went down with Nora Willett, and I can clear a lot of those up.

And because Nora meant something to me.

Maybe not to anyone else. But to me.

II

It began on Leah Parker's birthday.

I would say the typical things, like we had both gone to school with Leah, or that Leah was a friend, but you need to understand something about how Bethel works first. The entire town has a population of maybe five hundred, in a strong year. Leah was technically my friend in the way that everyone was technically my friend, but not in the way that Nora was my friend. Nora and I had gone to school with Leah because Nora and I went to school with everyone. My mother still has a picture of all two dozen of us, lined up in a row on graduation day. I remember Nora whispering to me that she was shocked that they even let *us women* graduate at all, considering how the rest of the town was. I smacked her so she'd shut up, but I did it right as they were taking the picture, so the image is tainted by Nora's serpentine grin and my arm brushing halfway across her waist.

The picture was taken a little over a year and a half ago now, but no one would let us forget it. That's how Bethel is. You do one thing that bothers someone, and everyone else seems to remember it clear as day, whether they were involved or not. Except, clear as day was never quite clear as day, and memory only went so far as you wanted to believe.

Leah Parker was a fine girl. She was simple, and a bit plain, but we were all happy to celebrate her turning eighteen. Eighteen is a big deal for Bethel girls because it is the age we are finally allowed to get married. Years ago it had been sixteen, but then the state yelled at us and threatened to arrest a whole bunch of people, so we changed it to avoid trouble. That's what Bethel is about, you know? Smooth it out, smile, and move on. I keep saying it, but I want to make sure you understand. Keep quiet. Stay out of trouble. That's why Nora was such a big deal.

The problem with the transition between sixteen and eighteen is that most of the time, a birthday is now accompanied by a wedding. Leah's birthday wasn't, but with the way Tommy McClain kept leering at her, none of us would have been surprised if a ceremony and then a pregnancy crept its way around the corner by the end of the year.

Nora and I had both turned eighteen earlier that summer, but neither of our birthdays had been met with half as much fanfare as Leah's.

The field behind the McClain farm had been entirely cleared out and cleaned, with a large table set up in the center, covered in cornbread and sausage and large bowls of red beans and rice. Sheets of white linen were hung up, blowing gentle in the October breeze. They caught the light and softened it, casting a heavenly glow on the entire party. If I hadn't already known I was at a birthday party, I would have assumed this was one of the special outdoor services we sometimes have, dedicated to celebrating the beauty of God's earth. It was that nice.

Nora and I arrived together, just a few minutes after everyone else. She always said that she preferred to arrive late because it made everyone notice her that way. We spent a few minutes milling about, got some food, talked to some people. Well, I talked to some people. Greeted Pastor David, as was proper. Sent my well-wishes to Leah, who was beaming in crooked-toothed delight. Nora just stayed, like she always did, a few feet behind me and to the left, where she could observe without interacting. Something about gathering information, she would say. I never pretended to know what she was talking about in situations like that.

Leah's eyes caught Nora, and her face fell.

"Abigail, I didn't invite her," she said to me in a low voice. "I didn't want her here."

I tried to stay polite, a smile stretching broad across my face.

"You invited all of Bethel, Leah. She's part of Bethel," I responded gently, not really wanting to press the subject much further. It wasn't uncommon for people to say *all of Bethel* and forget that included Nora too. What they meant to say is *everyone they like*. I don't know why they didn't just do that instead.

Leah's face twisted into a terrible expression, not too different from the sort you get when you put too much lemon in your mouth, or if a skunk gets you right in the face.

"Not *my* Bethel," she spat back. "It's fine. I'm sure she won't stay long anyway."

"I'm sure we won't." I nodded. "Happy birthday, Leah."

"Happy birthday, Leah," Nora echoed behind me, but her tone was far less kind. I was certain she'd heard what Leah said to me, but she didn't say anything.

I walked back over to her and placed my hand on her arm, smiling. Trying to ease the tension. Doing what I did best—acting as a buffer between Nora and the world. Nora didn't say anything then either, or as we walked away, silently agreeing to watch people from a distance.

We waited in silence for a moment, letting people come and go—congratulate Leah, joke with Tommy, shake hands with Pastor David. Social functions at

Bethel work more like a machine than anything else. An endless to-do list of things you have to remember, God forbid someone feels left out or forgotten. Nora picked at a stray thread on her dress, pulling it farther and farther out, unraveling it bit by bit.

"Stop that," I said to her eventually. "You're gonna rip your whole dress apart, and I can't fix it then."

She grinned, pulling the thread farther, pushing me just a little bit more.

"Bet Leah would like that, don't you think?"

"I bet not," I countered. She frowned, and we went silent again.

A few people looked over our way, back and forth between me and Nora, shaking their heads silently. They just didn't know how to mind their own business. At least once a week, a concerned neighbor was knocking on my mother's door, asking her if she knew just what her daughter and that heathen Willett girl were getting up to when the sun went down. We didn't actually get *up to* anything, whatever that meant, but wasn't that just the way? People got an idea in their heads about someone, a thought, burrowing deep in their brain like a maggot, and then all of a sudden it had to be the truth, no matter what facts or reason had to say about the whole thing. That Nora was bad, which meant that I was bad too.

At this point, we had been friends for too long for me to pass her off as my passion project. I used to tell people I thought I could save her, and the reason I spent so much time with her was because I was trying to help her get right with God. I don't really know how true that ever was, but I couldn't exactly tell them that something about her just called to me. That I couldn't tear my eyes away.

"There's a snake speaking to me, Abby-girl," Nora whispered in my ear after another long while. That's what she used to say whenever she felt like doing something she knew other people would disagree with.

"Nora, don't," I whispered back. "Please don't mess up Leah's birthday. Everything looks so nice." I don't know why I bothered to plead, considering she wouldn't listen.

"She doesn't fuckin' like me, I don't know why I should bother to be kind."

I turned to Nora, hitting her arm.

"Language," I hissed. "It's her birthday. Find some kindness in your heart for her, alright?"

"She didn't want me here, Abby. She made that clear as hell." Nora widened her stance, crossing her arms over her chest.

I'm fairly certain she mumbled something else under her breath, too, but I didn't hear her. I regret not asking, now.

"Well, you're here, and there's free food," I said in an attempt to placate.

"Free food and fake smiles, what more could a girl need?"

"If you could just—"

"If you tell me to keep sweet, I really will start acting up."

My mouth snapped shut; I didn't want to press her threat. It wasn't what I was going to say, but I didn't imagine she particularly wanted to hear me tell her to pray for peace either. I could only pray so much for the both of us, and I wasn't even sure if God would listen to the silent prayer that slipped out on instinct.

"I don't control you," I continued. It's important to remember that at this point, I didn't really think she'd actually do anything that bad. The worst we'd ever gotten from Nora prior to this were a few disagreements, one or two of them developing into a physical fight, and that nasty business with the snake. She was never truly a threat. At least, she hadn't been until this point.

Her face took on this unusual, contemplative sort of expression. I didn't often try to figure out what Nora was thinking, but I did in that moment. She didn't seem angry or bitter or anything like that. Nora's most frequent emotion was either anger or some sort of mischief, but I didn't see either of those in her eyes.

It wasn't quite sadness, either, which was quite rare for her. It was almost dancing at the edge of melancholy, with a bittersweet tinge to it. She had a smile on her face, but it didn't reach her eyes.

"You're not gonna like this one, are you?" she asked me.

"When do I ever like the things you do?" I replied.

Nora raised an eyebrow, seeming to imply something I couldn't quite understand.

"You do sometimes."

She didn't say anything after that.

I'm sure you've heard what happened next, but I think it would be best for me to describe it in the way I understood it to be. Lots of people like to blow things out of proportion for the drama of it all, or to garner more sympathy. What Nora did wasn't good, mind you, but it wasn't like she lunged forth like some wild animal, ripping and kicking and screaming.

She just walked forward, as if she was joining the birthday crowd. They were all singing now, presenting Leah with a well-made, plainly decorated pound cake. A few of them looked at her all suspicious, which they were right to do. Nora wasn't a joiner.

This is the part where things get mixed up. Most of the time, people will say that she lunged at Leah, nails out, intention to attack. There was a kind of fire in her eyes, some sort of vengeance, I suppose, but she didn't lunge. She didn't even move particularly fast.

She simply stood behind Leah, reached her hand out to grab a good solid chunk of Leah's hair, and slammed Leah's face down onto the table.

That's when everything erupted.

Leah pulled away from Nora, but Nora didn't let go. Instead, she ripped her hand backward, taking a large chunk of Leah's hair and scalp with her. Leah screamed. And I mean she *screamed*. It was the loudest, shrillest sound I'd ever heard, echoing around the whole field, joining the panicked yelling and shouting of the rest of the crowd. There was blood everywhere, gushing from Leah's nose, caked in Nora's nails where she had clawed at Leah's scalp. It might've been the most blood I'd ever seen in my life at that point. People were moving, frantic, desperate to figure out exactly what had just happened.

In the midst of it all, Nora stood still, almost as if in shock. Part of Leah's scalp still dangled from her hand, and she stared at it.

"Get her away from Leah!" someone shouted, and they began to move toward Nora.

This pulled her back to reality, and her once-blank expression morphed into one of pure pain.

"God, I'm so sorry," she said, dropping the largest of the scalp chunks to the ground. She fell to her knees, burying her face in her hands.

She wasn't sorry, though. I knew she wasn't. Every single thing Nora ever did was perfectly planned, even if she never bothered to tell anyone else what that plan might be. God forbid, someone might've tried to stop her.

Maybe I should've.

"I'm sorry, I'm sorry!" Nora kept shouting, over and over again, as crocodile tears mixed with the blood smeared across her cheeks. "I didn't mean to, I don't know what happened," she sobbed.

"The devil's in that girl," I heard someone behind me whisper. It sounded like Ruth Winsby, one of the women on the Bethel Pentecostal council. Figured. She was always the first to cast judgment, throwing attention on anyone who might have been considered unclean. Normally that just meant Nora, but sometimes it meant me as well.

There was no way to connect me to Nora's violence this time, so I was safe from criticism.

In the background, Nora kept sobbing as people whispered, throwing false prayers to the wind as Pastor David and his brothers, Elijah and Caleb, surrounded where she fell. Some of the other women had moved around Leah, checking her nose where it had surely broken, pressing the soft linens to the parts of her scalp where hair had once hung, soaking and staining them with blood. Leah was crying, too, but her tears didn't fill the air in the way Nora's did. Her presence didn't command the same attention as Nora.

I looked back and forth between the two of them, watching the women tend to Leah, her blonde hair falling in limp clumps around her, gashes gouged into her head. Watching the men hold Nora back as she wailed, moving her body about like some sort of wild animal.

Time went silent for a second as I watched her. I took in the smaller bits of Leah's scalp still clinging to her nails. The way the blood stained her fingertips. My mind wandered, wondering briefly what it might feel like to help her get it off. To scrub her clean, washing away her sins like she deserved.

As if sensing my thoughts, Nora's eyes met mine, and for the briefest moment, her face was dry. There were no tears. There were no sobs. Just Nora's wide, gleaming smile. She winked.

I keep coming back to moments like this. Wondering if I should have said something. Wondering if I had, would anything have changed? I doubt it. Nora would have still been Nora, and things would have still progressed exactly the same. I don't wish for omniscience. I just have a lot of regrets.

Pastor David pulled Nora away from the rest of the party as she cried and cried, begging for forgiveness. I wish I knew what kind of forgiveness she meant.

*

Nora and I became friends the same summer my father died. We were both seven years old, and it was the hottest summer Bethel had ever seen.

When it gets hot, which it often does this far down south, people tend to forget themselves. Never quite so bad as the people who live down in southern Alabama, but still. I don't pretend to know just how hot it was, but I remember how sticky. People joke often, they say things like *It ain't the heat that'll get you, it's the humidity*. But they aren't kidding. It covers the town, blanketing it in a wet, heavy air. Sometimes I swore I could see it, shimmering with heat, covering the asphalt in a dangerous sparkle.

Heat created anger. Boiling up under skin, until people were twitchy and ready to strike. Few things I remember about that summer aside from Nora and my father, but one of them was the sheer number of fistfights that had to be broken up. Everyone was so testy. And it didn't help that while tensions were high, people distanced themselves from the Lord, dressing less modestly to generate some sense of cool, and finding themselves far more willing to compromise on their original hard-held beliefs.

The devil had slunk his languid way into Bethel, so it was only appropriate that things happened in the order they did. It wasn't a coincidence that Nora found me, and that the course of my whole life changed with one conversation.

It happened the day after his funeral. My father's death wasn't a quick or an easy one, and it tore my family apart. I mean, obviously it did, considering he, my mother, and I were the only members of the Barnes family, and he never really liked me all that much anyway. He wanted a son. Someone strong that he could hand down the family name to.

After three miscarriages and years of trying, there I was. A daughter who could barely pay attention in church, let alone carry on the family name and faith.

He died, I think, of cancer. That's anyone's best guess. He refused to see a doctor, claiming that the Lord would heal him if he was meant to be healed. My mama let Pastor David in with all those snakes, and Elijah brought his guitar. They sang and praised and gave themselves entirely over, act of faith by act of faith, but still, it didn't work. He died unceremoniously and was put into the ground the very next day on account of the fact that the heat would have made the body smell worse. And the funeral was fine, nothing special really. It wasn't like Abraham Barnes was the most venerated member of Bethel society. Our community showed up, brought their flowers, said their prayers, and then he was in the ground. Nothing more than a piece of stone with his name and some numbers carved into it to indicate that he was ever actually a man.

I didn't particularly care. I was a little bit bored, but my father and I weren't close, so I was keen to go on my way and keep doing child things.

What I couldn't stand, though, was what came afterward. The morning after the funeral, dozens of people crowding our tiny two-bedroom home, dropping off food and sending their well-wishes my and my mother's way. The way they looked at me and whispered *Poor little girl, what'll she do now without a father*? I didn't want their pity. And I hated the way my mother soaked it up, tears staining her face like they would for months to come, accepting their hugs and support.

It wasn't that I was an unkind child, or that I had some sort of deep-rooted hatred for the people of my community. I just wanted to be left alone, you know? I just wanted to be able to process the absence in my life and my relationship with God without everyone getting all in my face about it.

So I snuck away. I darted out the front door when it swung open, passing another swathe of well-wishers before they could even notice me. I knew I wouldn't be missed. It was never about me, anyway. It was just about making sure my mother knew that you had shown up for her husband's funeral so that God wouldn't hate you for ignoring your community.

I found myself by the lake. My search for peace had led me to the water, which wasn't all that surprising. I liked the placidity of it, and the services Pastor David held outside were some of my favorites. Something about the way it held so much in such a small space—I couldn't wrap my mind around it. And people were rarely there—only for sermons or the occasional lakeside baptism—so I was more likely to be alone than anywhere else in Bethel.

Only, because nothing seemed to want to go well for me, I wasn't alone.

I can't even particularly say that I wasn't alone, because Nora was there first.

She was small, smaller than me, and more than ratty enough for me to be a little impressed. I always had respect for the dirtier people—the ones covered in a thin layer of dust and grime at all times. It meant to me that they didn't have anything to prove to anyone, which I guess says more about me than anyone else in Bethel.

The reason for her dirtiness was obvious enough—she was lying on the ground, in the sand-and-dirt mixture that lined our precious lake. Her dress—what had once possibly been a lovely blue color—had faded to an ugly, unusual sort of gray, like she hadn't been able to get a new one in far too many years.

I knew who she was, of course. It was hard not to. Nora Willett was commonly referred to as a *terror to the community*, but really she was more of a minor annoyance. A couple weeks prior to the funeral, she had gotten kicked out of our last day of school for sneaking a live worm into Leah Parker's lunch. Before that, she had gotten in trouble various times for shouting during church or making a mess of herself at the expense of someone else. It wasn't that her parents didn't care—they tried to discipline her. She just preferred not to listen.

I respected that about her, as much as it scared me.

Nora heard me coming before I had the chance to turn around and find somewhere else to go. Popping up from the sand like a crab, or a snake, she grinned at me.

"Your dad just died, didn't he?" she asked. I was taken aback and couldn't respond at first. Everyone had spent so much time dancing around me, dancing around the subject of my father, that Nora asking me point-blank when she hardly even knew me felt like sacrilege.

She took my silence as an indication to continue.

"That's sad, I guess."

"You guess?" I asked, walking past her to the edge of the water.

"Yeah, I guess. I didn't know him, but it's sad for you because he was your dad. So I'm sad that you're sad." I couldn't really come up with an argument for that, so I just stayed quiet. Nora dug her fingers into the sand, letting the grains burrow under her nails.

"Do you miss him?" she asked.

I looked out at the water, trying to figure out how to respond to her. On the one hand, yes, I did miss him. The absence of him was evident, and I had spent a good amount of the past few days wondering just exactly what I was supposed to do without him. But, at the same time, that absence was more clearly felt by my mother, who sobbed and sobbed at the idea that he would never return.

Absently, I wondered if I wasn't supposed to be happy for him. After all, did he not achieve what the rest of us were desperate to? Did he not reach salvation, and would be seated at the table of the Father for all eternity? He was, how they all said, in a better place. So why would I want him to return to a world of sin and misery?

"No, not really. He's where he belongs now, I think." I sat down next to her, grounding myself in the sand.

"That's good then." She nodded to herself. "I like your dress."

She didn't say anything else about my father, or about the funeral, or even about death. We talked for hours about everything and nothing, from her deep love of snakes and the forest to my secret hatred of Pastor David's longer sermons (which was a feeling I was delighted to learn that she shared). Nothing was out of the question, and for the first time in my life, I felt as though anything I said was completely and perfectly safe. Nora was the only person to grant me the respect of honesty, but also of secrecy.

I didn't leave until the sun was setting, and I could hear my mother calling for me across the way. When I told Nora that I had to go because I didn't want my mother to worry, she sort of just laughed and shrugged, suddenly seeming much wiser and more dangerous than any seven-year-old had a right to be.

"Go then." She smiled. "I'll see you tomorrow."

After that day, we became inseparable. No matter what we did or who we crossed, we were glued at the hip, and no one else could change that. I don't spend much time wondering why we chose each other so fiercely, but if I had to put a meaning to it, I think it's because she didn't care. She was so young, and none of it mattered to her. Not the church, not Bethel. She was content with only herself, and I coveted that carelessness for my own. I orbited her like she was the sun, and probably would have whether she cared about me or not.

You're not here about all of that, though, so I'll keep on with my story.

III

After the party, everyone was more than a little bit wary of Nora Willett. And for good reason too. Leah was sporting a pretty gnarly bald spot, not to mention the fact that the McClains had traveled over to the Willetts' to request proper compensation for the damaged property. There wasn't actually much damaged property, but it was the principle of the thing.

Nora's mother didn't really do anything about what happened, and her father was away on some trip or other like always, so for the most part, we continued as normal. There were calls for Nora to be put into a holding cell, or for her to be tried for assault, but none of it came to fruition. In the end, people prayed about Nora, and Leah was left looking embarrassing and patchy.

The only thing they could truly force her to do was go to church and hope that her soul got saved, which she didn't particularly mind because when she was at church, she stood with me.

Our church was run by three brothers—men who some would call the pillars of our community. The most in charge of the three was Pastor David; he was the oldest of them, probably around forty-five years of age. I had gotten used to seeing him around from the moment I could understand what going to church meant, and everyone in Bethel was practically in love with him. People said he looked just like his father, Amos, but I never knew the Taylor patriarch, so I formed my own opinions. He was a bit ugly, with too-long limbs, a too-thin face, and hair that fell in yellowish strings right above his eyebrows. He looked like maybe he had spent one too many hours out in the sun, with redness and blisters across his cheeks, but had none of the bulk or strength to show for it. It was evident that David wielded the power of the Lord well, and that power might have been some of the only strength he would ever receive.

After Pastor David, there was the slightly younger Elijah, who was perhaps thirty-six or so. Elijah was sweet, for the most part, but tended to get too deep into the communion wine on occasion and lash out in pretty nasty ways. Before she died, Esther Carthage was supposed to marry him, and he never quite recovered.

People said he'd been handsome once, but I couldn't understand what they meant. He was much bulkier than his brothers, and most likely very strong, but he kept to himself, preferring the company of his guitar over the company of another person.

And then the baby of the Taylor family, Caleb. Caleb was the most upsetting of them all, not in the way that David or Elijah had their faults, but more that he genuinely liked to torment people. It wasn't uncommon to hear Caleb uttering the tense reminder that *we were all going to hell anyway*, or to watch him pull a rattlesnake from his coat pocket just to frighten a child. Caleb was the snake handler of Bethel Pentecostal, and that was only because no one else would dare to do it. A terrible man of about thirty years old, Caleb had small, beady green eyes, and a tongue that darted out from between cracked lips with enough frequency you'd think we were in a drought. We joked a lot that Caleb was more snake than human, but looking at him made you question whether or not we were truly being serious.

All three of them worked together to run the services; David giving the sermon, Elijah providing the background music, and Caleb sitting in wait for anyone who might dare to want to prove their faith.

The sermon the week after the party was no different, though it had evolved some since the beginning of the service. David had invited us to join him in worship, calling out to the Lord as we all saw fit. Naturally, this shifted into a cacophony of people speaking in tongues, singing, making up hymns of vaguely suited words to go alongside Elijah's aimless guitar plucking. Caleb had even retreated to the sacristy to gather some of his favorite snakes for those who felt holy enough. It was a madhouse of faith, but I'm certain that if Nora hadn't done anything, it would have gone down as one of the more successful services of the year. Normally, the church's success was limited to Easter and Christmas, with those being the days that the most people showed up—sometimes even a few people from the surrounding towns through the mountains, if they were brave enough. That day, there weren't any out-of-towners, but almost everyone born in Bethel had gathered to listen and to learn lessons. Our hearts were open to God, which meant that at the end of the day, people were more likely to believe David when he had something to say, or to take his side in an argument.

Of course, there had to be something. I wouldn't be telling you about this if there wasn't.

As the people all pushed forward, desperate to be close to the music, to the snakes, to anything they could think of that might prove their worthiness and get them into heaven, Nora and I hung back, and my attention was pulled away from the parishioners.

"There's a snake speaking to me, Abby-girl," Nora whispered behind me, about halfway through the service. Only, her voice didn't carry that mischievous tone it normally did when she was going to do something terrible. She sounded scared. She sounded overwhelmed. She didn't sound like herself at all.

I turned to look at her, half expecting it all to be an act, and her face to be plastered over with that stupid smirk.

But it wasn't. She looked just as afraid as she sounded, and torn as well. As if she had a choice to make, but she desperately didn't want to have to make it.

"Nora . . ." I whispered back nervously. "What's going on?"

Before us, the parishioners continued to worship, the thick, rolling sound of tongues permeating the air. They writhed like their own form of snake, like they had all become one person, one cloud of humanity, desperate for the Lord's love.

Nora didn't say anything. She shook her head, reaching her hand into her pocket and taking hold of something. I hadn't paid particular attention to her pockets before that moment, but if I had, maybe I would have noticed the wiggling. The writhing. The indication that there was something else there that I needed to look at—needed to stop.

But of course I didn't stop her, you know that.

I just sat silent as she pulled a beautiful baby copperhead from her left side, letting it twirl between her fingers like it was her very best friend.

My mind traveled back to a moment in the forest—many, many years prior—and I stilled with fear.

"Nora," I whispered again, but her eyes had glazed over like she was concentrating hard on something, "put it back."

She didn't.

She dropped it, and it sped off into the masses, vanishing almost as quickly as I had seen it.

The first scream came quick. Quicker than I expected. The shrill sound broke through the crowd's shouting like a siren, and Rebecca Winsby—Ruth's daughter—came stumbling out, clutching her ankle like she was dying. A grin split Nora's face, and I knew she had reached her target. At least, one of them.

Here's the thing about copperhead venom. It isn't very potent. It isn't even normally deadly. The worst it can do is cause some tissue damage and pain for a while, lots of swelling if you're particularly unlucky.

Maybe Rebecca Winsby was particularly unlucky, or maybe it was something else entirely, engineered by Nora's mind and her mind alone, but it was far more than just some simple swelling and tissue damage.

Rebecca teetered away from the crowd, her face already half-gray. Her ankle was where the bite was located, sure, but the veins in her neck were a dark navy color, and she looked like she was choking, struggling for air like she had never known how to breathe at all. At her ankle, the skin was almost black—cracking in places and oozing a yellow pus. She was rotting from the inside, like the copperhead itself had infected her with more than just a simple venom.

I watched as she moved farther from the masses, past me and closer to Nora. As she passed, the thick scent of rot filled the air, and I had to stop myself from gagging. Rebecca was decaying, and there was nothing anyone could do about it. At the corner of her eye, a drop of blood began to pool, and it spilled out of her tear duct, tracing down her face like a ruby tear. Rebecca wiped it away, smearing the blood across her cheeks and nose. Eventually, she reached Nora, and her legs must've given out at that point, because she fell to her knees before the other girl.

I couldn't hear much over the sound, but what I heard Rebecca say to Nora still lingers in my head sometimes to this very day.

"Please," she whispered, her voice hoarse, "help me."

Nora's grin split even wider, to the point where I thought her cheeks were going to tear just to accommodate it.

She didn't help. She didn't say anything. She just brought her hand up, reaching for heaven, and then with a movement quicker than I thought possible, she brought it back down with a sharp *smack* to Rebecca's cheek.

Rebecca collapsed, but not before I caught a glimpse of what had become of the cheek that Nora hit. The skin had been displaced, tearing away from the bone itself, ripping like soft cotton. Rebecca's face was falling away from her skull, and Nora was smiling.

Rebecca screamed as she died, but no one turned away from Pastor David and his sermon.

Elijah was the next to go. He was the one who really stopped everything because how could they continue to sing if there was no music to go along with it?

He didn't scream the way Rebecca did, but he let out more of a pained groan—a wail of injury more than of fear. Much of the same happened: his face went that pallid gray color, and the veins on his neck bulged an uncomfortable dark blue. David turned to him in a panic when the music stopped, and when he turned, the sound of the worshippers quickly faded out. I couldn't see where he had been bit, but I assumed it was near the feet as well, something quick and simple for Nora's copperhead to access.

Elijah mumbled something in a frantic, breathless tone, and David looked scared.

"What is it, brother?" he asked, moving to Elijah's side.

Trembling, Elijah raised a hand and pointed our direction.

"*Nora!*" he screamed, and his voice rang out through the church, and, I'm certain, through all of Bethel. That seemed to take all of his energy because he collapsed almost immediately after; becoming nothing more than a heap of useless, pus-leaking flesh that could barely even breathe without struggle.

People haven't stopped speculating about those deaths, and I don't think they ever will. Their favorite thing to talk about is just how impossible the whole thing was, that maybe Nora poisoned the snakes, or maybe she had poisoned their minds with her demon-powers, whatever those ended up being. They ignore the fact that Rebecca Winsby was already potentially ill, and that Elijah Taylor had maybe gone into some form of liver failure from drinking too much alcohol. They all would rather talk about what Nora did and didn't do, making up more bullshit that didn't even sound like anything she could've pulled off.

Which is exactly why no one was paying attention when Elijah finally died. They were all glued to the sight of Nora Willett, holding the baby copperhead once more, and grinning like the day she was born.

She wasn't paying attention to them. Her snake had returned to her, and I had to wonder if it was the very same snake from before, years ago in the forest—the same one that she had taken care of, and that owed its life to her.

She held it up to her face, pressing a gentle kiss to the edge of its snout. The world watched as Nora implicated herself, right then and there.

David stood above it all, above the bodies and the tears and the blood, glaring at Nora from across the silent room. He said nothing, but his expression alone was a promise—no, a threat.

He would do something about it.

The problem of Nora Willett would be handled, and if it wasn't solved, it would be ended.

Nora's grin did not fade.

*

There are a number of events that might've led up to the church moment, if one wanted to create a timeline of Nora Willett's life. I bring this up because I know you're going to ask me, and I'd be the most likely person to know—especially considering her mother rarely paid her a lick of attention save for shouting at her when she did something wrong. People like to ask lots of questions like that, things like *who could have seen this coming*? And *what would have led the demons to take over such a poor young girl's body*? Or *she was so innocent, why Nora*?

I've got a pretty distinct idea of the things that might've led Nora to become possessed, if *possession* is the word you're choosing. Nothing typical, not like speaking in languages she didn't know or vomiting up thousands of bugs. She didn't do none of that. She did some pretty violent and terrible things, and I'm happy to talk about those to clear the air, but what everyone else is missing are the subtleties. The things I promised her I'd never talk about, or the things that other people might look over.

This is one of them.

I can count on one hand the number of times I'd seen Nora actually sad. You'll probably hear about most of them just from this tale alone, and one or two of them are secrets that I swore I'd never tell. But the first, though . . . the very first, was when we were about ten. The forest was humming its mournful tune around us, and we thought we were completely alone. No one is technically alone as long as there's God, but there's an absence that comes with being around Nora, where you're not really sure whether or not God even matters.

We found ourselves in the forest instead of our oft-ventured spot by the lake because Pastor David was setting up there. It was a Saturday afternoon, and he was set to be preaching in our regular hangout the next day, so we didn't want to get caught. We abandoned the water for the trees, and on that day, we were better for it. I liked the forest just fine, with no particularly strong feelings either way, but Nora loved it. She told me it felt like a second home to her, the way the trees were bending and groaning in the wind, and the twigs and leaves crunched underfoot.

She could disappear there, she said. It wouldn't even be hard.

I didn't entertain her talk of disappearance or abandonment because I didn't want to even come close to the idea of life without my best friend.

We walked for a while, occasionally in silence, occasionally mindlessly chatting about whatever had happened in school the past week. It was nice, a peaceful sort of quiet that we didn't usually get in Bethel, but it ended, as all things tend to, with Nora.

She stopped in front of me, holding her hand out to stop me as well. There was a sharp inhalation of air, and then her entire expression changed, as if her world had been shaken with just one action.

"What is it?" I whispered, not wanting to break the tranquility of the moment.

She didn't respond, just took another step forward. Crouching down, she reached her hand out toward a small pile of dead leaves, wrapping her fingers around something that I couldn't quite see. When she rose again, what she was holding became far clearer, and my heart stopped.

It was a snake. A copperhead, to be specific. We could identify them easily around Bethel, considering how frequently Caleb Taylor used them in his brother's services, but also just because we saw them a lot. They made their homes under rocks and by our houses, and from the moment I learned to walk, I could remember my mother telling me to watch where I stepped, just in case the devil had put one in my path to test me. The bites—while ugly—wouldn't kill us, but at the end of the day, a snake bite never meant anything good. It meant that we'd have to admit that we'd gotten close to it in the first place. That we were out where we weren't supposed to be, and then we might not have been allowed to ever come back.

My instinct was to smack it out of her hand in fear, but that probably would have caused it to bite her, so I just froze.

I do a lot of hesitating, you'll find.

It took a second for the actual scene to register, and for me to understand what was really going on. The snake, which Nora held close to her heart as if it were a child, was not moving. It wasn't even twitching. Where it might've once posed a threat, this copperhead was limp, and its head was hanging on to its body by barely a few strings of flesh and bone. No snake at all would have been best, but a dead snake was better than a live one. Someone had most likely seen it and killed it on a hike, worried about the danger it posed to the campgrounds in the mountains. I let out a sigh of relief, but Nora wasn't quite so easily comforted.

A tear rolled down her cheek, and I marked the moment as the first time I had ever seen Nora Willett cry.

"What do we do?" she whispered, stroking the snake gently with her thumb. "We can't just leave it out here."

"It's dead," I said, my voice flat. "There's not much we can do at all."

She frowned at me, and I was left feeling like I had failed some sort of test.

"I won't just leave it all exposed. That isn't fair." She adjusted her hands so that the snake was spiraled within them, and if I didn't pay attention to the way its head was more than a little severed, it might've looked alive, like some sort of pet.

"Okay, we can bury it then, I guess." It was the only thing I could think of, but it seemed to satisfy Nora, who immediately knelt to start digging. Placing the snake by her side, she dug her hands into the soft earth, creating a small hole.

"Aren't you gonna help?" she asked, turning back to me. I nodded, moving to help her dig the hole deeper.

It's one of God's creatures, even if I don't like it, I told myself. *It deserves a fair burial and protection.* Still, it made me nervous. All snakes did. Something about the way Caleb Taylor handled them in church, like I would never be quite good enough to prove my faith and one of them could bite me at any minute during the service.

I didn't like it.

After a few minutes, the hole was dug, and our nails were caked black with soil. Nora picked the snake up once more, cradling it close. I heard her whisper a few words as she did, but I couldn't make out what she was saying. It didn't seem like it was really for me, so I didn't press. This is one of the rare times when I don't wonder what she said because I know that even if I'd understood her, nothing would have changed.

Expectant, Nora turned to me.

"Do you have anything you want to say?" she asked, holding out the snake. I sat for a moment, trying to come up with something that was tender, respectful, and still appropriate.

"Um . . ." I paused. "Rest easy, snake. You deserved better." I didn't reach out to touch it, even though that's what it seemed like Nora wanted me to do. She could handle the touching and holding of the thing. My words were enough for me.

Nora pulled the snake back to her chest, whispering again. She stroked its head, not seeming to notice where the head was separated and became strings of blood and flesh. She ran her thumb along the body, handling it with such tenderness that I almost felt jealous.

Maybe it was an act of desperation, or maybe she just wanted to afford the snake a shred of dignity, but before she placed it in the ground, she pushed the head back onto the rest of its body. Her hands were trembling.

It looked real again.

She cradled it, just above the hole in the dirt, and right before she opened her hands and let it fall, the snake twitched.

It moved.

The skin between the head and the body shuddered, and then knit itself back together like it was only a few threads that had kept the poor thing from being alive in the first place.

Time was suspended among me, Nora, and the snake for what felt like hours. We watched in a sick combination of fear and awe as the snake continued to twitch, and to knit, and to come back to life in Nora's hands.

Neither of us really believed it until the copperhead slithered out of Nora's palm and twisted its way around her wrist like some sort of bracelet.

I held back a scream, but Nora's jaw just hung open, and her eyes held the faint twinkle of a smile.

"It isn't dead." Nora laughed. "It isn't dead!" She held the snake up, letting it play amongst her fingers. It didn't lunge to bite her, didn't seem to even want to consider how dangerous this whole thing might be.

"You–" I stuttered, "you brought it back."

She did. That couldn't be denied. With whatever power she had in her little ten-year-old body, or whatever demons she was capable of reaching out to for help, Nora had brought the snake back to life.

At that, Nora's face fell, and she dropped the snake to the ground. Within seconds, it moved away, forgotten and scared, but newly alive. Heart beating. An abomination.

"We can't tell anyone about this," she whispered, her eyes still on the copperhead darting away into the leaves. "You can't tell anyone about this." She shifted the emphasis onto *you*, as if she expected me to be the one to do something. Admittedly, I was afraid, but my loyalty to Nora seemed to outweigh my fear of the church.

"I won't," I promised her.

She took my hand, squeezing it fast.

"You have to swear to me that you won't, Abigail." She looked into my eyes. "No one can know."

The fear was thick in her voice.

"What'll they do if they find out?" I asked, scared to know, but wanting more to understand what she was so afraid of. I was still of the age where I assumed the church would understand and help, as untrue as that ended up being.

"They'll kill me." She whispered it, but the echo of the words still bounced off the trees. "They'll burn me for witchcraft, or try to deliver me, or maybe even both of us, if they knew you were here too." Glancing back over at where the snake was, she let out a shuddering breath. "We can't tell anyone."

She was right.

"Promise me." She took my other hand, the dirt mixing between them and smudging across our skin.

"I swear," I whispered, my voice as grave as I could make it. "No one knows."

This was the first secret I kept for Nora Willett, but it wouldn't be the last. I collected information about her, holding it close to my chest, consuming the secrets like the most precious of fruits. I didn't think about what it meant that the snake seemed to revive itself with Nora's touch, or exactly how much she whispered to the creature before it all happened. It didn't matter. What mattered was that I had her, and that there was more that brought us close.

IV

After the incident at church, my mother very calmly informed me that I wasn't allowed to be around Nora anymore. It wasn't any sort of big, blowout fight between the two of us—my mother isn't like that. She remains polite and quiet, no matter what. But she wouldn't accept an argument, which made things difficult on my end. She simply sat and watched the entire process of my emotions, moving from my understanding, to my sadness, to my frustration and anger, without ever once batting an eye. Sarah Barnes is not a negotiator.

She told me that after everyone had left and everything had been cleaned up, the Bethel Pentecostal council had officially diagnosed Nora with possession, and that I couldn't be seen around someone who hadn't been saved.

I bet you didn't think a diagnosis was part of the process, did you? Well, it is.

Possession is a funny thing, right, because technically, it *is* a mental health issue that *can* be diagnosed. Your mind has been damaged far past the Lord's control, and demons have been let in. Whether you are or aren't actually possessed, you at the very least have to believe that you are, and therein lies the problem.

Everyone seemed to believe with their whole hearts and minds that Nora was possessed, despite the fact that she had never claimed it, or even mentioned a demon or the devil or nothing like that at all. It was the simple matter that the Lord didn't move through her in the way that he moved through everyone else, and that was enough.

There was no point in arguing with my mother after she had made her mind up, so I didn't. I sat quietly, finished my bible study, and then told her I was going to say my prayers and go to bed.

Don't you wish it were just that simple?

No, things with Nora were never that easy, and I could never give her up just like that. Everyone else could, maybe, because they were all itching to move on to the next best thing, but not me. She stuck on my brain, some might say like a leech, but I prefer to think of it like syrup.

I never could remove her all the way.

So instead of saying my prayers and going to bed, I found myself climbing out of my window and dashing down to the lakeside, well after sunset, after God and everyone had all gone to sleep. Don't ask me how I knew I would find her there. It was just what made the most sense. It was where she spent the majority of her spare time, often just staring out into the water like she expected something to reach out and grab her. Maybe that's what she wanted.

If you were to ask anyone, they'd all tell you I shouldn't have gone. They'd probably say something about how dangerous she was, about how she had caused the deaths of multiple people at that point, and that she deserved to be locked up. But none of that was ever directed toward me. I never felt danger around her, and I knew, somehow, deep in my soul, that Nora wasn't going to hurt me.

So it was easy enough to approach her the moment I reached the bank—I didn't even stand around trying to decide whether or not it was a good idea. If anything, I hesitated just for a moment because of how startlingly beautiful she was in the moonlight.

Because she was.

And it isn't a sin for me to call her beautiful, either. It's just the way that the moon reflected off her hair, changing the soft brown into streaks of perfect silver, and how the light reflected in her eyes, turning all of Nora into some sort of beacon for me to gravitate toward.

She was lying out by the water, her arms by her sides and slightly out, almost like she was sleeping. But her eyes were wide open, and she was staring at the sky like she had never seen anything so vast, so dark, so . . . promising.

She moved when she heard me approach, and I cursed my loud shoes and the grass for ruining the moment. Sitting up, she was poised to dart, as if she hadn't wanted anyone at all to see her, let alone her best friend.

But when she realized it *was* me, she relaxed, patting the soft patch of sand beside her.

"It's a pretty night," she said, curling her arms around her knees and drawing up into herself. I hated her like that—all closed off and empty. I couldn't understand her then.

"It is a pretty night," I agreed, coming to sit at her side. And it was. We were reaching the end of the summer, which meant the thick, weighty heat that plagued us before had softened, becoming awash with cool breezes and the promise of an eventual autumn. There were fewer clouds, because there were fewer storms, which meant that the sky was peppered with perfect stars.

I wrapped my own arms around my knees, half in an attempt to mirror her, but half because I just didn't know what else to do. We sat like that together for a while, watching the reflection of the moon on the lake, not acknowledging anything that had happened earlier in the day.

I'd let her talk when she wanted to, but I wasn't going to risk the sanctity of the moment by making Nora feel unsafe.

Eventually, she moved closer to me, until our arms and sides were almost touching, and I itched to close the distance.

"What are they saying about me, Abby-girl?" she asked, resting her head on my shoulder and closing the distance herself.

I thought for a moment about keeping it a secret and not telling her anything that my mother had told me, about the church, about her diagnosis, none of it. I'm sure I was never supposed to share that information at all, but her mother should have known, considering Bethel was what it was. Someone was bound to find out sooner or later. But still. Possession was such a big thing, and it *was* Nora's possession after all. Did she have any right to know what the church was going to do to her? Maybe I should have left it all in God's hands.

My silence was far too long, or far too loaded, because Nora turned to look at me, her eyes a little too wide for her face.

"What is it?"

"They've diagnosed you with possession," I blurted, knowing that if I said it faster than I thought it, my mouth wouldn't let me take it back. I feared a negative reaction from her, maybe fear, or dread, or something to indicate that she was still herself in there, still a God-fearing young woman who knew what her priorities were (those, of course, being her God and her people).

Instead, she laughed. It wasn't a real laugh, instead sort of hollow and hopeless, but it was different from what I expected, which was startling enough.

"Do *you* think I'm possessed?" she asked me, a danger in her voice. I didn't ever know what the right answer was with her, which was frustrating. Did she want me to say yes? Or would saying yes make me part of the church, part of what was going on deeper within Bethel?

"I think you don't know what you're doing," I admitted. I didn't know exactly where to stand on the whole possession thing. Sure, she had caused pain, and death, and all sorts of other things, but she always had! It wasn't helped by the fact that I couldn't quite get out of my head the idea that maybe the church just wanted to be rid of her altogether and couldn't think up a better excuse.

"I think you're at least right about that." Nora sighed. She reached for my hand, tangling our fingers together, and I said nothing about how warm her skin was, or about the thrill of her touch.

"Aren't you scared?" I asked her, desperate for any shred of what might've been going on in her mind.

"Not really, I don't think. Just tired." I could hear it in her voice when she mentioned it. The exhaustion. The weight of everything, pulling her down and away from me.

"Why do you do it, then? If it makes you so tired?"

"Do what?"

I didn't know. Cause problems? Start fights? Argue?

"Sin," was the answer I settled on. It made the most sense. An umbrella term, under which many transgressions could be categorized. All of Nora's badness could be summed up into that one simple word.

"Sometimes you have to remind people what they're fighting against for them to realize just how stupid it all is," she replied.

That was beyond me. I couldn't tell if she was calling the church stupid, or all of Christianity, or what any of it meant.

"They're going to perform a deliverance for you." I changed the subject, not wanting to implicate myself further. "It'll be like—"

"No, it won't. Stop talking about it."

I shut my mouth, a little bit hurt. I was just trying to warn her. Trying to remember the last time something like this had happened, and all that resulted from it. I didn't want Nora to end up hanging from the rafters of a barn, pale and cold like—

Well, we won't talk about her yet.

I didn't want anything to happen to Nora at all, but she seemed insistent on making sure something did, so the very least I could do was warn her.

"I'm sorry." Nora sighed again. She could tell her words had hurt me. "I'm just . . . too wrapped up in all of this, I think." She curled her fingers into mine, running her skin—rough, tanned—against my own—soft and pale. On instinct, I wove our fingers together and squeezed, tight.

"You don't have any demons inside you really, do you?" I asked. I had to be sure. I had to know that she would be safe, and they had no reason for any of this. It was just precautionary.

Nora laughed.

"Not the ones they think they're looking for, no."

I didn't lose myself in the fact that it wasn't a full denial, and maybe somewhere deep in her brain a demon *had* taken root. I just let the relief wash over me, taking her word for what it was, because it was worth everything to me.

No, I don't regret that, before you ask. I trusted her implicitly. She gave me no reason not to.

"Thank the Lord for that, then," I said, the relief evident in my voice.

She laughed again, and I joined her. It felt nice to have this moment of peace, where we could just exist with each other and not have to worry about anyone else seeing, or telling me to stay the hell away from her, or reminding me that my duties were first and foremost to the Lord.

We fell against each other in our laughter, our bodies blurring together in the darkness. When I looked at her, I could see the stars reflected in her eyes, and I knew that there was nothing that she could request of me that I wouldn't do.

When we finally became quiet again, the weight of the night settled on our shoulders like a heavy fog.

"Can I do something stupid?" she asked, the last of the joy leaving her voice along with the words.

"When don't you?" I replied, trying to regain some of the teasing tone that had defined so many other moments of our relationship.

She frowned. "Abigail, I'm serious. Can I?"

I nodded, because even if I didn't particularly know what Nora wanted to do, disagreeing with her or forbidding her from something wasn't in my nature. It was always so easy to give her what she wanted, and she took it with grace.

She twisted her body, turning until she was facing me. I've told you I didn't know what was coming, but still, the nerves pooled in my stomach like a coiled wire, electricity crackling at either end of me. I faced her, too, and let her reach up, taking either side of my face in her hands.

"Don't kill me for this, okay?" she asked, a tense laugh breaking its way through the words.

"I couldn't," I responded, too honestly.

She leaned her head forward and kissed me.

Her lips were chapped, bitten down and maybe a little bit bloody, but that didn't matter. Mine were a far cry from soft, anyway, and it wasn't like I was trying to impress her.

It was brief.

I wished it wasn't.

I wished I had taken her hands and kept them there, pulled her face closer to mine, lost myself in her touch and let the moment suspend itself eternally so that neither of us ever had to go anywhere or acknowledge anything outside of that kiss. But I didn't, and it ended.

She pulled away first.

"I'm sorry, I don't know why I did that," she said, shaking her head.

But she was lying. We both knew why.

My hand traveled up, touching the place where her lips had just been, needing to capture that feeling and keep it forever.

"You—" I started to say something, but I couldn't finish.

Nora shook her head.

"Don't say anything." Her hand came to rest on my arm, and she gave me a gentle squeeze. "It's okay."

She looked around the lake, taking it all in.

"I need you to know that I can take care of myself, Abigail." She paused, collecting her words. "If something happens to me, I'm going to be alright. But *you*,"—she looked at me again, directly—"you need to be careful. Watch yourself closely and know when to run."

She pressed another kiss to my forehead, this one less intimate, more similar to the kiss Pastor David gave to the recently baptized. I still wanted to keep it, though. I wanted to cling to her touch and pull her closer and closer and closer to me until we were utterly indistinguishable from each other.

Instead—coward that I am—I sat and watched in silence as she rose and walked away, back toward the church and our homes and everything that felt so wrong and broken.

I let my hand travel back up to my lips, wondering exactly what she had wanted from that kiss, or why she had even been so nervous about it to begin with.

*

She had done it once before, but neither of us seemed to want to remember that. To be fair, I probably wouldn't have wanted to remember it either, if I had been in her position.

We were thirteen when it happened.

Also by the lake, if you can believe it. I guess it might've been a prime spot for kissing teenagers, if people hadn't been just so damn scared all the time.

A couple of years before I was born, people used to come to the lake all the time. There was still a boathouse on the shore as evidence, though now it was hardly safe for anyone to even get close to, let alone keep boats in. They'd picnic on the shores, spend the warmer days swimming in the water. Back then, Pastor David would deliver sermons by the water almost every other week, weather permitting. It was a place of celebration. Of joy.

Until, that is, two kids decided to get stupid and tip over a boat in the middle of the night, drowning themselves underneath it.

They'd gone out for . . . inappropriate reasons, I'll say, and no one even heard them scream.

The next morning, their bodies were found washed ashore like gifts from the deep.

People had pretty much avoided the lake ever since, save for Pastor David's bimonthly sermons at the water. I think that's why Nora was drawn to the lakeside so much. The death behind it. The fact that people avoided it. Maybe she felt bad for the lake, wanting to keep it company like I did. Or maybe she just enjoyed it because of the dark reason people never lingered, and wanted them to associate her with that sort of danger.

Anyway.

I found her there after school, sitting like she always did, sand in her hands. She hadn't been in our last few classes of the day, disappearing around lunch, so of course it had been my mission to find her the moment I was free.

And find her I did, as she was angrily tossing clumps of hardened beach into the water, watching them disperse and float down to the bottom.

"Are you alright?"

She jumped when I spoke, which then caused me to

start as well. It wasn't like Nora to be jumpy, and it was even less like her not to anticipate my arrival.

"I'm fine, Abigail." I didn't like it when she used my full name. There was something tense about it, like she had pushed me to her periphery with the rest of the world, refusing our closeness. Testing the boundary, I placed my hand on her shoulder. When she didn't move, I sat down next to her, close enough to feel the warmth radiating from her body, but not quite touching.

"I didn't see you in Bible class today." It was the reason I had gone searching for her, like I said. I worried about her, despite all her fearless anger. Nora was still a person, even though she seemed determined to convince us she wasn't.

She shook her head, but I couldn't tell if it was genuine or if she was mocking me.

"No, I left after lunch. Leah and her parasite decided they wanted me to see what hell on earth actually feels like."

She was referring to Rebecca Winsby. Rebecca stuck to Leah's side much like Nora stuck to mine, but they were far less interesting about it. Rebecca was also the most annoying person by far in Bethel, going out of her way to make sure that everyone knew just how much she knew about God.

It was no wonder she and Leah were so conjoined, what with Leah's insistence upon her own perfection.

"What happened?" I didn't want to ask her if she

was alright again. It would only make her mad.

Nora sighed, shaking her head again.

"You don't need to worry about all of that, Abby-girl." She plastered on a fake smile, turning to me. It didn't reach her eyes, but I didn't say anything about it. "I'll be just fine, like I always am."

"Was it about your father?"

Silence fell between us.

There was an open secret in Bethel that Nora's father wasn't exactly the most righteous of men. He didn't always stay in the community, traveling around to places like Birmingham and Atlanta. He would always come back with something new, something unholy. Her mother didn't say anything about it, but the parishioners went wild whenever he was back in town, whispering that he was an adulterer, that he was a homosexual, all sorts of nasty things. Nora insisted he just traveled for work, but no one in Bethel ever traveled for any good reason, so it was likely she was lying.

He was a decent enough man, the few times that I had seen him, but I couldn't help but wonder if he actually cared about Nora at all. I mean, it wasn't like he hurt her or anything like that. Worse things had happened in Bethel before. He brought her gifts from far away, and she idolized him to hell and back, but he wasn't even there in the end. Never once did he recognize that she needed help, and never once did he stay.

He wasn't connected to anything in Bethel, though. Especially not his family. He just drifted through like it was a place to land when he needed, like Nora was something to be entertained when he had to, and something to be forgotten when he was somewhere else.

She ate it all up, though, whether he cared about her or not.

A few days before Rebecca made her comments, he had returned home once more with a bag of mysterious books in hand for Nora to read. She had shared a few of them with me, but none of them were to my taste. Too much questioning and mystery, the kind that made my chest go tight.

"I think Rebecca's exact words were *Be careful, Nora, or you'll end up on the side of the road like one of your daddy's whores.*" Once she said it, her lips tightened, and her fists balled up like a threat. On instinct, I felt my own hands go tight, and I knew at that moment that if Nora asked, I'd get any sort of revenge she wanted.

If I hadn't been so much of a coward, maybe I would've gone with her in the end.

"Well that's bullshit," I said, summoning the worst of words that my young mind could muster. "Your father is a good man, and it's their fault they don't know that."

I crossed my arms, hiding my balled fists. Nora relaxed a little bit, slumping so that our skin finally touched. I didn't lean into her warmth, but I was suddenly very aware of it, little jolts of electricity running between her arms and my own.

I wondered if it was wrong to think about how pretty she was when the sunlight hit her eyes, all while she was telling me something so terrible. The way her lips formed words was indescribable to me, and I lost myself while she talked.

"I don't want to think about it" was what she said. But I didn't hear much of that. I just nodded, agreeing with her that *yeah, we shouldn't think about it, let's do something else.*

There was a shift in me then, that I don't like to think about very often. Nora moved from being my closest, dearest friend, to something so much more than that. I had lost our friendship in that moment, but in its place, something entirely new had grown, and I loved that even more. I saw her differently, I touched her differently, and in the back of my mind, I pushed away the fear that any of it might've been wrong.

It was fine, as long as it remained in my head. That's the way it goes. Everyone thinks about sinning, but it's a matter of whether or not you act on it. And I wouldn't! Like I said at the beginning of all of this, I'm good. I know how to behave.

Everything else is on Nora.

"Your brain is somewhere else," she said, grounding me once more, forcing my eyes away from her lips and her arms and the tan of her skin. My brain *was* somewhere else.

"Sorry. I was trying to think about . . ." I couldn't come up with a lie quick enough. "Other things?" It wasn't good enough, and Nora knew it.

She smiled, though it was still a little bit sad.

"Yeah, okay, Abby-girl." She leaned into me more, strengthening the connection between the two of us. I wrapped my arm around her, in a show of girlish solidarity, and not because I wanted to pull her even closer.

But closer and closer she came, until our faces seemed to smash against each other, lips meeting in a collision of skin and confusion. It was, in that moment, the most perfect thing that had ever happened to me, even if it is a little ridiculous to look back on. We were children, and neither of us knew anything, so we definitely looked a little bit silly, and the sand wormed its way over our skin and into our hair and clothing.

So much for not acting on sin.

She pulled away from me, and I felt her absence immediately. I didn't say anything, though I think both of us wished that I had been brave enough to pull her back.

We sat in silence for a moment, and I tried to think of what to say. What to do. If there even was anything.

I didn't wonder about hell and damnation until later that night in my bed, when the thoughts crept back into my mind and her face seemed to be the only thing I could think of.

I tried to tell myself it wasn't right.

I tried to force myself into repentance, right then and there.

I never did anything about it, though.

Did she actually mean to kiss me? Did she actually want to? It was always an easy choice for Nora, whether or not she wanted to do something that other people might not have liked. She didn't ask me to keep it a secret like she had all those other times she'd done something wrong. She didn't ask me to hold it close to my chest, and think of it only late in the night, after God and everyone had all gone to sleep.

I did, all the same.

I captured those memories, pushed them all into a pretty little jar deep in the back of my mind, saving them for only the worst of times, when I was at my saddest, or when I wanted to hold onto pieces of myself that no one else would ever understand.

Because that's what Nora was, wasn't she?

A piece of myself that I couldn't explain—or maybe didn't want to explain, and now she's been carved out of my heart, and I'm never getting her back.

V

The day of Nora's deliverance, the weather was terrible. It was only a few days after our kiss by the lake, but it was like the seasons had decided to shift entirely, and the sky opened up, pouring every single inch of saved rain it possibly could. It was hot, too, which didn't help. The air was wet and sticky, causing our clothes to cling to our skin, and our hair to run in strings down our faces as it was made heavy by the water.

My mother washed my best dress for church that day. I should have known that something was happening, but they didn't tell me exactly what was on the schedule. I didn't know when the deliverance was supposed to be, only that it was going to happen soon. A number of other things could have indicated the purpose of the service to me, that now I think maybe I was just too dumb to recognize.

My dress.

The fact that Nora didn't walk in with her mother when she arrived, and that her mother arrived looking somber, yet hopeful.

I looked around for her, confused and frantic, but there was no sign. Even Nora didn't skip church, no matter how much she complained or made it everyone else's problem.

And then there was the fact that when Pastor David addressed us, he told us that we were going to do something very, very special that day. Something that he considered a game changer in the eyes of the Lord, something that would improve this community and the people in it beyond our wildest dreams.

I see that look on your face. It sounds real suspicious, doesn't it?

But no, it was just her.

I say *just* her. It was never just her, and the look on my face must've been a sight to see in that moment. Caleb pulled her out of the back room, shoving her to her knees as Pastor David began the sermon. I would tell you exactly what he said, but to be honest, I don't know.

I wasn't thinking about God. I wasn't thinking about the fate of my soul.

I was only thinking about how scared she looked. And how sad.

She must've sent Nora in the night before, her mother. I wondered if her father knew anything about what was going on. If he would've done anything, had he been there. He seemed to be so above it all, content to let his wife take the reins on their daughter's life. All he had to do was sit back and make the money, leaving Nora in the hands of the people of Bethel to do with as they pleased.

And look where it had gotten her.

She looked like she hadn't slept. Her hair was knotted and ratty, and her dress was wrinkled and dirty. Caleb looked much the same, so I figured he had probably stayed up, praying over her as they sometimes did with the most at-risk of cases. I shuddered to think about Nora and Caleb alone in a room together, him with the assignment of preparing her soul for salvation. He looked pleased with himself.

She looked haggard, with dark circles under her eyes and a glazed-over, tired look to them as well.

She met my gaze and didn't say anything, but just sat there. Staring. Pleading.

I felt a tear roll down my cheek before I could do anything about it, and I shook my head.

"I'm sorry," I whispered. It was lost in the noise of the crowd.

"It's okay," I saw her mouth back. "I'll be okay."

I didn't believe her.

"It isn't often that we get the opportunity to directly influence God's will," Pastor David spoke, pulling my attention back over, "but today is one of those days. Today, we will get to have a hand in saving the soul of this poor young girl, lost in the grasp of Satan himself!"

He paused for dramatic effect. There were gasps in the crowd. I'm fairly certain I heard someone scream. Nora rolled her eyes, and, also for dramatic effect, took a big breath in and spit directly on his shoes.

It didn't help her case.

Caleb stepped forward and smacked her, square in the back of the head. Out of the corner of my eye, I saw her mother flinch and turn away.

What were they thinking?

Did they really believe that this was the only option? Were her parents so blind to everything around them that they thought this was the only way to save their daughter? A man with some snakes and another on a power trip?

"Nora Willett is troubled, but we have the power to save her, together, as a community!" Pastor David shouted. "Nora needs Bethel, and we will do everything in our power to bring her back home!"

"I am home, you stupid fuck!" Nora shouted after he was finished, her words punctuated by an awful laugh. Her voice didn't sound like her own. It was raspy and pained, like it was coming from somewhere else entirely.

Caleb reached forward again, raising his hand, but David stepped in front of him, blocking the blow.

"What Nora needs is her people, and her God," David said. Caleb rolled his eyes but backed away. I've never in my life wanted to punch anyone more than him in that moment.

"I invite you now," David continued, turning to the crowd, "to come forward and help me save Nora Willett's soul."

That was all it took. The congregation surged forward, hands raised to the heavens, ready and willing to do their part.

I didn't move.

My mother looked at me, her face accusing, and I smiled softly, clasping my hands together as if I was going to offer up some silent prayer.

I wasn't, but it did the trick. She turned back toward Nora, fighting against the crowd of people trying to get closer and closer. To touch her—put their bare hands on her skin and pray like they actually cared about what happened. They covered her completely, and I was forced to drop my gaze. Their voices came together, a mixture of prayer, hymn, and the ever-present vibrance of someone speaking in tongues. I wasn't quite sure who felt drawn toward the Lord enough that day to lose the English language, but the sound threaded through everything else, landing on my ears in a harsh melody.

Outside, a thunderclap sounded, and lightning cracked off in the distance. The rain pounded heavy on the tin roof in its own sort of rhythm. I jumped at the sound of the thunder. Normally, it wasn't like me to be so easily frightened, but there was something in the air that morning that made me uneasy. I felt like a rubber band, pulled far too tight and ready to snap.

There was a brief gap in the crowd, and I saw Nora once more, her face pointed upward to the sky. I doubted she was thinking about heaven, though. It seemed more likely to me that she was wishing for lightning to strike the building and stop this whole God-damned ceremony.

Next to her, I saw Caleb, standing smug, as if he had something to say.

He must've, because as everyone moved and writhed, he bent over, slowly getting nearer and nearer to her face.

The crowd swarmed again, and I lost sight of her. I tried not to panic.

My eyes were locked on the image of Caleb leaning down. Close—too close—to Nora's ear, and the wicked grin that crept across his face as he did so.

What could he possibly have to say to her?

Nothing that would end well, surely.

After a moment of not seeing her—not seeing Caleb either—something changed. The scent of blood was heavy in the air, but I couldn't exactly tell where it had come from. It wasn't Nora—if she had been hurt, we would have all known.

That dreadful, pained silence filled the air, and I caught sight of both of them once more.

Nora on her knees. Caleb lying before her.

Caleb was a sight to see. His body was slumped on the ground, resting at her feet. If it hadn't been for the gaping hole at his throat, and the blood covering the rest of his body, I would have thought he was sleeping.

The first scream came from Nora herself, which shocked me more than Caleb's body. I watched her face contort into something almost inhuman, and the shriek that came from her torn-open mouth made my ears bleed.

David was the next to make a sound, which didn't surprise me. He had already lost one brother, and there went the second, so quickly, at the hands of the same girl. He was alone.

The last remaining member of the Taylor family stood above the parishioners, face contorted in an expression of sorrow.

The sob didn't last long, and I'm only half convinced it ever happened. He pulled himself together in a blink, and I watched as his expression glazed over with one of brutal, relentless anger. He was never the kind of person to be outwardly violent—it was easy not to be when you had the might of the Lord behind you—but I could feel the tension in the room, the brimming heat through righteous veins. His anger twisted into a smile, albeit a sad one, and he turned his calculating eyes Nora's direction. Not spitting venom, not calling for her capture, but letting her scream. Letting her cry. Letting something else brew in the place of the punishment she would've received if she had been anyone else.

Quickly afterward, the entire church erupted into a cacophony of sound, screams and sobs echoing through the building. Nora herself led them, holding her blood-covered hands against her cheeks, smearing the blood across her face and clothing, mixing it with the tears as she had done with Leah's. I could see what had happened pretty clearly, then. She must've pulled Caleb close to her when he had bent down to whisper, and, using a combination of her bare hands and teeth, ripped his throat clean out of his neck.

Below her, and in front of everyone, Caleb was still. There was no doubt in my mind that today was the very last time we would ever see him handle any sort of snake.

Maybe it was for the better.

Or maybe it wasn't. A man was dead—again—and it was—again—Nora's fault.

I looked up at her, wondering if I should be sobbing and screaming like the rest of the crowd. Like her. I didn't feel any sort of way about it, which felt wrong, but there was nothing I could do about that. I wasn't going to lie and join in just because I felt like I should. I looked at Nora, searching for any sort of guidance, desperate to see if she could give me some clue as to how she wanted me to respond.

Her open-mouthed screams had taken shape, and words were forming on her lips. It took a moment for me to decipher their meaning, what with everyone's reaction to the body and the blood, but after a bit, her voice took hold over the crowd.

"*I'm saved*!" She was screaming, but it sounded almost like a hymn. "I'm saved, you did it! Everything is fine and He is here!"

Over and over again, she kept repeating, "*I'm saved. I'm saved.*" Like Leah's birthday and the repetition of her *please.* She was desperate to convince them to leave her alone.

And they did. They backed away from her, almost as soon as they could register what she was saying. They stood back in awe as she held her arms out over Caleb's body, rising to her feet, dripping blood like rain.

"*I'm saved.*" Her voice came out in a rasp, but it was the most perfect sound I had ever heard. She looked at me, an awful sort of twinkle in her eye, and she smiled.

The Lord will surely forsake me for this, but I must admit that part of it was . . . well . . . beautiful. I don't know whether or not she was actually saved, but something about the way the blood shone in the light, and the way her smile seemed to be only for me, no one else in the room . . .

I wanted to walk up to her.

I wanted to wrap my arms around her and take her home, protecting her from everything undeserved until the end of time.

I wanted to do more for her than her family ever had. Make promises that I knew I was unable to keep, whisper things that I knew would surely send me to hell.

I couldn't, though.

My mother wrapped her hands around my arms, forcing me backward out of the church. I didn't lose Nora's gaze as she did so, desperate to hold on to what was left of my friend.

"I'll find you," Nora mouthed, as I was pulled away from the crowd, away from her. "I'll find you."

I wish I could say that it was only comfort I felt in that moment, but no.

The idea of that did scare me as well.

*

I should talk about the other deliverance. The most recent one before Nora. We don't do them often, right, because we're so isolated down here that sin to that degree isn't frequent enough to necessitate it, but she was different.

Her name was Charity Fuller, and hardly anyone remembers her. I wouldn't remember her either, if not for everything that came after. If not for Nora. The people of the congregation seemed to remove her name from their memory not even a month later, though. It's because she wasn't saved, I think. She didn't quite make it, and Bethel likes to wash away mistakes like that.

We were fifteen at the time, and there was a lot of speculation about Charity's deliverance, especially because of the nature of the service. Everyone was being so vague about it, and a lack of information allowed rumors to spread like kudzu, wrapping around our throats and forcing the words out against our will. Some people said she was pregnant, which is why we needed to pray. Some people said that Betsey Allen was involved, whore that she was, and had convinced poor sweet Charity to sin alongside her. Whatever the case, the deliverance was a big deal, and every single God-fearing person in Bethel was there that day, desperate for the glory of helping save Charity's soul.

And because it was the first deliverance in just about three years. That sort of thing was always monumental. We all gathered in the cool conditioned air of the church as Pastor David felt the glory of God coming through him, and Elijah plucked out a solemn hymn on the guitar.

"We are all children of God, are we not?" He liked to begin his sermons with a question. It drew everyone in, he said. Made them start to think.

The crowd murmured in agreement. Of course we were children of God, what else would we be?

"And as children of God, we can do powerful things through him, can we not?" The audience murmured again in response, slightly louder, more powerful. The attention had been gotten.

We all knew that we were there for a deliverance, of course, but the lead-up was one of the best parts.

The guitar continued, low and resonant as ever.

"Today, my friends, we will have the opportunity to put that power to the test!" he proclaimed, tossing his hands up in the air. The congregation cheered, delighted at the chance to prove that they could do all things through Christ, who strengthened them.

"There is a lost lamb," Pastor David continued, "and it is our job to help her find her way home, as Jesus would if He were here. She has sinned, and sinned again, and now it is the responsibility of her church and of her community to step in and help her get right with God." He sighed—a heavy, false thing—and clasped his hands together. "Now if you'll join me in a moment of silent prayer."

The whole church fell silent, sending up their individual prayers for the lost lamb of God. An energy ran through every person present, a tension practically screaming for Pastor David to just get on with it, just get to the good part.

On my end, it was mostly dread, mixed with a healthy amount of hope. Deliverances were a good thing. Deliverances brought us closer together. But they were also horrifying, in a beautiful way. Watching the sin get stripped from people's very bodies and having their faith tested in remarkable ways—the Lord was mysterious, and I wasn't quite sure that fear was the route that should have been taken, but nevertheless, I sent up my own silent prayer and waited.

A shuddering sigh of *amen* rippled through the crowd, and Pastor David looked up at us all once more.

"Brother!" he called, motioning over to Caleb, who had been standing by the door. "Bring her out!"

Caleb Taylor pulled Charity out by her hair. It was pathetic, really, and probably one of the first indications that they had never actually intended to *save* her, just show her off until she wasn't their problem anymore. She looked half-starved and rabid, like they had been keeping her in the basement since her indiscretion had occurred. Her wide eyes wandered the congregation, searching for something. I tried to follow her, to see where she was looking, but she never lingered on one thing long enough for me to understand. Falling in stringy lumps around her face, Charity's hair was knotted and tangled, like no one had ever once bothered to brush it.

Most likely, her parents had turned her in the night prior, forcing her to stay up with Caleb and Elijah and David, sitting in silent prayer. But silent prayer shouldn't have made her look like that.

I tried to remember if she looked that bad before.

Maybe it was the devil that made her that way.

I didn't know.

I looked to Nora, tried to see if she was watching with my same sense of surprise—tried to guess what she was thinking.

Her eyes were downcast, and her mouth was pursed in a pained way. If I didn't know better, I would have thought that she was trying not to cry.

"This child," Pastor David's voice boomed, pulling my attention back to the pulpit, "has sinned."

Well, obviously. The thought leaked into my mind before I could control it, and a small giggle escaped my lips. Nora's eyes darted upward, meeting mine. Her expression seemed to beg me for some sort of relief, and I offered her a tense half smile. She didn't return it.

The plucking of Elijah's guitar continued, providing a low ambiance to pull us through the sermon.

"Young Charity here might've forgotten the Lord, but the Lord has not forgotten her." Pastor David's voice bounced off the wooden walls, and we were still. "But we can save Charity!" he shouted, causing some of us to jump, breaking the stillness he had created. "She is still a child of God, whether she wants to admit it for herself or not! She will be healed, and the Lord will move through us today!"

Charity was deposited on the pulpit, Caleb pushing her downward with more force than was probably needed.

"I now invite you, members of this beautiful congregation, to come and bless Charity's recovery." Pastor David held his hands out, magnanimous as any man of the Lord could be, beckoning us forward.

I felt my mother's sharp elbow dig into my side, shoving me forward. I didn't want to move, but my feet pushed forward without my consent, as if it was all I could do.

I wasn't the only one moving forward. There were several people: Charity's mother, a few girls from our class, Leah Parker—anyone who wanted to seem as faithful as they could in the eyes of Pastor David. My mother trailed behind me, not because she wanted to help deliver Charity, surely, but to make sure I was doing the exact right thing.

And I would do the exact right thing.

I walked up to the edge of the pulpit, waiting my turn while Pastor David shoved Charity's head forward to the parishioners, making her more of a pathetic mess than she already was.

"Father, help us deliver this girl from evil!" he proclaimed, raising his free hand up to the sky—the taller he was, the closer he was to God, of course. "Help us remind her of what truly matters! Help us to recover her faith and bring her home!"

His voice continued as I approached, echoing a number of reminders, of praises, of threats. I couldn't tear my eyes away from her, how sad she seemed, and I began to ask myself what it all was worth.

If it made Charity hurt like this, then how much did God's love really matter?

Almost immediately, I tensed, casting the thought from my mind.

We were saving Charity.

She was saved.

This would make things better.

She just didn't realize it yet.

When it was finally my turn, I was hopeful. God was all-powerful, and I knew that, and Charity needed to accept that He could save her.

My eyes reached hers, and that hope immediately shattered.

There was nothing but hatred there. My hands were hesitant, and I almost didn't reach out to her in fear that she might try to bite me. Charity, as upset as she was, looked at me like I was a thing to be ruined, or like I was the one doing the ruining. I knew in that moment that she wanted me destroyed, but I couldn't quite figure out why. Was she looking at everyone that way? Or was it just me?

Her skin was warm, or maybe mine was just cold— I'm unsure, but either way, they were two things that were never meant to meet. I whispered a quick prayer, promising both to Charity and to God that she could still be saved. But it felt useless.

All of it felt useless if Charity hated us anyway.

I returned to my seat, watching for whatever came next. As numb as I felt, it was the only thing I could do short of getting up and leaving, which no one would have tolerated. After everyone was seated once more, Pastor David whispered a few words to Caleb, who had been standing off to his left just behind Elijah. Caleb smiled, reaching behind the podium and bringing forth a small cardboard box.

From the box, Caleb pulled one of his favorites. Her name was Delilah, and she was reserved for only the most special of occasions. She was a timber rattlesnake, a full-on adult, measuring at just around four feet long. Her scales rippled and writhed in a beautiful chevron pattern, and her tail vibrated with the holiest of sounds.

Seeing her, Charity's body tensed. She began to writhe and pull as well, eyes wide, mouth contorting into a terrified *no*. Pastor David held fast to her, though, keeping her situated there on her knees, holding her still in a way that was sure to bruise.

"No," Charity begged, her voice growing louder, meeting the volume of Delilah's rattle. "No, please, forgive me." Tears welled in her eyes, and my chest constricted at the sight.

"He'll forgive you, child. Put your life in His hands," Pastor David assured her. "Give your life over to Him. Prove your faith."

Caleb moved forward, Delilah curling in his arms.

"No, please, don't—" The tears spilled, and Charity's voice became nothing more than incomprehensible sobs as Caleb reached her, placing Delilah like a wreath across her shoulders.

She shook, her body folding over with fear, and I wanted to scream. To tell her not to move, to hold still until they decided that her faith was enough to let her rejoin the congregation. I felt a hand against my back, and I didn't need to turn to know that it was Nora.

Delilah curved around Charity's neck, claiming Charity as her very own, wrapping and wrapping until I could hardly tell the difference between Delilah's scales and Charity's hair.

I couldn't watch anymore. I shut my eyes, maybe in anticipation of a bite, a scream, or the proclamation that Charity was a true sinner who deserved to die, I didn't really know what to expect.

But the bite never came.

Delilah dropped off of Charity's shoulders, pausing only to hiss once at Caleb before darting quickly underneath a table across the pulpit. She didn't even linger on Charity, didn't once consider biting or maiming or anything. She was gone.

And then it was over. The service ended as soon as it had begun. Charity's mother grabbed her by the arm and pulled her out of there, the both of them bent over with tears but for entirely different reasons.

I stood, frozen, wondering exactly what it was that I had just witnessed. I couldn't measure my disgust, then. But now? There's a weight heavier than I can ever try to explain that hangs over that day. I don't know if it's because of what happened to Nora, or because of everything else, but I won't ever forget it.

Four days later, Charity Fuller was found hanging in her family's barn, all the life gone from her eyes. A cow had been eating one of her shoes, they said. That's why they found her. The cow brought the shoe right to the front door, and Charity's mama screamed and screamed.

I didn't need to ask Nora if she had heard about Charity's death. I didn't even need to assume. It was evident in the way her shoulders hung when I found her by the lake, hair falling in dark waves around her face, concealing her expression from me.

I had never once seen Nora pray, even when we were in church. She always just pretended, sometimes even going so far as to make silly things up or pray to false gods instead. I knew it wasn't right to let her do things like that, but I certainly wasn't going to stop her.

That day, though, shortly after the news broke, Nora was kneeling by the water, hands clasped, whispering something under her breath that I couldn't decipher. Not that I wanted to. It felt wrong to try to listen in.

I waited until she was done, until her lips had come to a full stop and silence fell once more before I spoke.

"I didn't realize you knew her." My voice came out in a whisper, partly because I was trying to maintain the serenity of the moment, but also because something about Nora seemed tense. Like a wild animal, ready to flee at any second. Nora just shook her head.

"We only spoke once or twice. I just . . ." She trailed off, and I didn't think to ask what else she was going to say.

"My mother says that Charity was a whore, and that she was caught kissing Betsey Allen behind their pigsty." I didn't say anything about how Betsey hadn't been seen since then, and that my mother told me that apparently her family had shipped her up to Kentucky, where supposedly there's a good Baptist Church that deals with *girls like her*. I didn't know exactly what *girls like her* meant, but my mother said it with a warning look in her eye, like she dared me to challenge it.

"Yeah, well, your mother will say whatever it takes to get Pastor David on her good side, won't she?" Nora brushed me off, venom in her tone. "The moment Charity's dead, it's like she isn't even human anymore, and you can say whatever the hell you want about her."

"I didn't mean it like that, Nora," I responded, suddenly feeling like I had done something wrong. And I didn't. I just wanted to connect to her, in the same way that the other girls in the village connected with each other. Trading other people's secrets like the most valuable thing in the world, snickering behind fences while watching other people intently, waiting for even the slightest misstep so they could run and tell all their friends what they saw.

"Don't you have any damn compassion, Abigail?" I blanched at her use of my full name. "A girl killed herself because *you all* made her feel like she wasn't right, and you're sitting there spreading gossip from your mother." Nora huffed, crossing her arms and turning away from me.

It was the *you all* that got me. I had been present at the deliverance, of course, but I didn't really know Charity. She was a few years older than us in school, maybe seventeen or eighteen at the time of her deliverance, but I had never even spoken to her. I couldn't have been part of it, right? Sure, here I was trying to tell Nora any sort of gossip I might've heard, but . . .

I remembered the way Charity looked up at me when I placed my hands on her, praying for her soul. There was hatred there, but the root of it had always been sorrow. I remembered Nora, mouth pursed, refusing to approach. I remembered the uselessness of it all.

Deliverance, despite what you might think, was supposed to be a good thing. It was supposed to rid someone of their sin, allowing them to become a new person. To get right with the Lord. It was never supposed to be sad or angry, but Charity and Nora saw it differently.

I see it differently now, too, of course. And I saw it differently for Nora's. But it had never been quite so easy.

"I didn't realize you felt so strongly about it, Nora. I'm sorry," I said softly. She didn't look at me, and I think that's because if she had, I might've seen that she'd started crying.

"I'm scared, Abby-girl," she whispered, her voice a harsh scar against the quiet of the lake. Despite that,

I leaned into the comfort of her using the nickname, finally feeling like we were on equal footing again.

"You don't need to be scared. We've got each other, don't we?" I didn't really understand why she was scared, but it became my job to comfort her. To fix it, and to promise that I could make the fear go away. She turned suddenly, facing me with the gravest expression in her eyes.

"Do you remember the snake?" she asked me suddenly. I looked around, checking to see if any people might've been within listening distance.

"I thought we promised not to talk about that." I let out a nervous laugh. "Why?"

"You remember it, though, don't you? And how we promised not to tell?" I nodded. She continued, "So you have my back about that, don't you?"

Was it some sort of twisted exercise in trust that she had chosen to ask me about it in that moment? We shared many secrets, Nora and I. The snake was just one of them. But there was a frantic, desperate energy behind her words, like she wanted to tell me something but couldn't figure out exactly how to get the message across.

For the briefest moment, I thought back to that night by the lake. How she had kissed me, and how I had kept it to myself—so very to myself that I wasn't sure even she knew about it anymore. That memory seemed more important than the snake, but I didn't say that. She didn't even ask me to keep that one a secret.

My lips tightened into a thin, stiff line, and I looked at her, nodding gravely.

"I always have your back, Nora," I promised. She smiled again, finally. A breath of air let into the almost suffocating moment. I didn't know exactly why she wanted me to promise, but I knew it was important to her. I knew that by doing so, I had secured our fates, entwining our very souls together until the end of time.

"Good," she whispered, more to herself than to me. "Good." I watched the fear leave her body, and I wondered what it meant for Nora Willett to be scared. What had she and Charity both known about Bethel, and what made not just the deliverance, but God Himself a thing to cower from?

The trouble was, I didn't have her back, did I? If I had, we wouldn't be in this situation, and I wouldn't be telling you all this.

VI

For a period of days after her deliverance, no one saw Nora. Not even me. Pastor David declared her deliverance a success, despite everything, so the lie her mother told was that she just needed time to heal and recover from all of the events. Bethel itself needed time to heal, too, from yet another loss at Nora's hand. But no one was ready to talk about Caleb yet, and even fewer were ready to admit that maybe we'd be better off without him.

Even fewer understood, or could even admit aloud, that maybe the reason David had declared her such a success was because he was planning something far, far worse for her in the end.

I was despondent during this time, refusing to talk to anyone, barely leaving my room. I was nothing more than a bundle of nerves—exuding pure, potent worry for the state of my friend. I didn't believe the deliverance had been successful, especially after the end of it. I wasn't even sure if I had agreed with the possession diagnosis, and I was certain Nora wasn't going to argue for or against it either way.

For the most part, my mother was relatively understanding during this time. While she didn't necessarily enjoy our friendship, she still understood that Nora was important to me, and that I was dealing with a lot of confusing feelings. She left me alone, and I left her alone, and we were even.

On occasion, she would make a vague attempt at comforting me, saying just the wrong words in just the wrong way. I appreciated the effort, and was always certain they would have been comforting words to any other girl in Bethel. But they never meant much to me.

This was how I ended up sitting on my bed, responding to a knock at my door.

I didn't tell her to come in—I didn't need to. She did whether I wanted her to or not, because there's no such thing as true privacy in a Bethel family home.

"You doing alright?" she asked, and I had to hold back a laugh. "I know these aren't the most ideal of circumstances, but things will work out in the end. God knows what he's doing."

This had nothing to do with God.

I didn't say that, though.

"I know." I sighed. "I just am worried about her."

"Why, honey? Why worry, when you know Bethel is going to take care of her? She's in good hands." *Good hands*. I held back another laugh. The hands of David, who hated her? The hands of Leah Parker, who'd kill her the moment God said it was okay?

"I just don't think this is deserved, you know?"

"Not deserved?"

"I think there are ways we could have gone about helping her without all of . . . this." I waved my hands around. The deliverance. The rumors. The whole show of it all. No one had needed to die. If Bethel had just made room for Nora Willett, it all would have been okay.

"She's possessed, Abigail." My mother was matter-of-fact, like this was the only fact she had ever known for certain.

"I'm not sure about that." I tried to remain as confident as I could with those words, but it was hard. My mother was on the council that had diagnosed her, and to question it would be to question the council's authority as a whole.

"You don't think Nora Willett has a demon in her at all?" She sounded like she didn't believe me, which I didn't necessarily blame her for. The evidence of her transgressions was astounding, not to mention, I'm certain my mother would do anything to maintain how correct she had been.

I thought back to the dead snake in the forest all those years ago. How Nora had cradled it, and how it had twitched back to life in her hands. I thought about her hands against my skin, how soft and easy we moved together. Her lips against my own, and the water around us. I thought of the fire that lit inside of me, even after we both left and the moment was over. More sins than I could ever name or count, all piling up around me, all because of her. Was she a demon? Did she have the devil in her?

I looked back at my mother.

"No," I said with absolute certainty. "She just needs guidance. Some people just need a little more work to be saved, you know?" I tried to offer her a weak smile, but she didn't quite buy it.

My mother sighed, gently petting my hair.

"I envy your heart, Abigail," she responded. "I'm just not sure it's wise to see the best in such terrible people."

"The Lord believes that even the worst of sinners can be saved, Mother." But even that felt like a lie. Despite what logic told me, despite the fact that people had gotten hurt—people had died—I couldn't make myself believe that Nora had sinned. And if she hadn't, then what was the purpose of her deliverance? Her pain?

None of it meant anything. Their reaction was pointless, and it only served to amplify whatever they wanted, not what the Bible wanted.

My mother didn't respond to that with much more than an agreeable *hmm*. She was satisfied with my answer. She was satisfied with the way that she had raised her daughter. Silently, I willed her to leave my room and let me get back to my yearning in peace. I had given her what she wanted, while still defending Nora, and it was high time I was left alone.

She seemed to pick up on my hint and rose from her place on my bed.

"That's enough of all this talk." She sighed again, dusting off her skirt. "I'll have dinner ready in a few hours. You can come get some or not, it's up to you."

And that was that. It was the last time my mother spoke to me of Nora, even after everything. She never bothered to ask how I was feeling after Nora vanished. She doesn't acknowledge how far Leah's gone to avoid me in the months since, like I've got some kind of Nora-plague, that I'll be the vessel for her second coming. It's just how she operates.

She left, and I was alone again with my thoughts, which weren't much better.

In the few days after the deliverance, when I had been alone, of course I'd been thinking about Nora. Worrying about her. Not quite frightened of her, but something close to it. I just didn't understand, and it seemed like the easiest way to get back to my friend was to just talk to her to try to figure out exactly what was going on in her head. There wasn't much actual luck of figuring out anything, with the way that Nora was, but I could dream. I could hope that maybe one day she'd trust me enough to be fully transparent, so that I could defend her in the best ways, and convince Bethel that she wasn't something to be feared. She just wasn't really like the rest of them, and that was fine.

After a few minutes, there was a *crack* against my window.

I froze.

There was another.

Crack.

Crawling over to my window from my bed, I swung it open, letting in the cool night air.

I was hoping for a branch, or maybe some sort of annoying bird, but instead of any of that, Nora Willett stood in front of my window, holding a small rock, poised and ready to strike.

I let her in before I could think about what I was doing. Seeing Nora was an exercise in instinct more than rationality, and she was slipping through my window before I remembered that she was a murderer, that the devil was in her, that there were a thousand other reasons not to hold her close or think about kissing her again. I had to hold myself back from hugging her, but even then it was because I wasn't sure she wanted to be hugged, not because it might've been dangerous for me to do so.

Reality came flooding back relatively quickly when

I heard my mother reciting a prayer in the next room. She was a *murderer*. There was blood on her hands. I stepped back, trying to mold my face into something that might've seemed like disapproval.

"I don't want to talk to you," I said, but it was a blatant lie. I was so relieved to see her, and I'm certain I didn't quite do a good enough job at hiding it.

"Then why'd you let me in?" she asked.

I had no response.

A smile—albeit a weak one—pulled at her mouth, and she wrapped me in a warm, tight hug. The sort of hug you'd give someone after not having seen them for months.

When we pulled away, my chest felt tight, and I suddenly found that I had so many more questions than answers.

"What are you doing here?" I asked, checking her over. She didn't have any marks like she was hurt, and she didn't particularly seem like she was in a hurry. She just seemed like she wanted to be here, which filled me with a strange sense of pride.

"I didn't know where else to go . . ." At that, my heart stuttered. You'd think that after so many years of being so close, I would get used to the idea that Nora was my friend. It never quite settled, and I was always a little bit in awe of her.

Still, though, it was dangerous for her to come. Not just for me, because my mother would raise hell if she found out that I was harboring a murderer, but for Nora as well, who might not make it out.

"But why here?" I asked. "You know that if my mother found you, she'd kill you herself."

"I wouldn't deserve it."

There was a pause between us, and I had to admit to myself that she was right. She didn't deserve any of it, especially not what my mother thought of her. But the least we could do was try to set things right. Try to understand exactly what was going on, and maybe even try to find a way to fix it.

"You need to explain yourself, Nora." Yes. An explanation would solve everything.

Nora frowned.

"It's more complicated than you think." I didn't know if she meant just Caleb and the deliverance, or the situation as a whole. I'm sure it could apply to both, which was especially frustrating. I didn't often get upset with Nora, but this was one of those times when I was running out of patience. If I could fix it, why wouldn't she let me?

"Well, make it simple then." I crossed my arms, waiting for her.

"I had to kill him." She lowered her voice, "Abby, I *had* to."

"Why?" I asked. "Because the demons told you to?"

She shook her head, drawing her mouth into a thin, sharp line.

"Because he told me he was going to kill me."

Silence fell between us, and I felt guilty for jabbing her in the way that I did. I didn't put it past Caleb to say something like that to her. To push more and more snakes toward her face. Even to threaten to strangle her. He probably would have grinned and whispered something like *Don't worry Nora, the Lord will grant you breath if you're truly worthy.* I remembered seeing him lean down, his cracked lips far too close to Nora's ear for my own comfort. I assumed he was just whispering a prayer, but if there was more—

Out of the corner of my eye, I saw Nora wring her hands together, exhibiting something that—if it hadn't been Nora—might've looked like anxiety.

"I'm scared, Abby-girl," she whispered. I flashed back to the other deliverance. I thought about Charity, and the only other time I'd heard her say those exact words.

"What did he say to you?" I asked. "We can try to talk to Pastor David. We can tell them it was self-defense. We can—"

"Oh, like they're gonna believe anything *we* say," she snapped, her voice growing louder and harsher. I recoiled from her, not out of fear of any sort of demon, but because I felt like I didn't recognize my friend.

"I am just trying to help."

Nora softened, placing a hand on my arm and rubbing it gently.

"I'm sorry, Abby. I know you are. It's just real easy to feel real hopeless now. I know they don't want me if I'm not some perfect, Godly woman. And after Caleb . . ." She shuddered. "I'm worried about what they're going to do."

"What did he say to you?" I asked again.

Drawing her knees to her chest, Nora frowned.

"He told me that David would kill me for what I did to Elijah. That he might as well get it over with now, and that he'd be doing his brother a favor." She shut her eyes tight, and I grabbed her hand. "He told me to look out at the people. See the faces of everyone participating. And know just how badly they all wanted me to die. That he would be God's favorite if he did it right then, and everyone would love and appreciate him. I—" She cut herself off, taking a deep breath. "I don't know what happened after that. Everything went black, and when I came back, it was . . ."

Underneath her nails there was still the faintest stain of blood, even after these few days. She balled her hands into fists, and the blood was gone from sight.

"Yeah," I said, mainly to get her to stop talking. I was there for everything else. I didn't need her to describe Caleb's body again, or the way the crowd reacted, or her voice ringing out in the silence, desperate to prove to us just how much she had been saved.

"I think this is it." The words felt heavy, like an admission. "I don't think I'm making it out of this one."

She leaned back on my bed, pulling the blanket up under her chin.

"Of course you are, Nora." I lay down next to her. "They can't do anything to hurt you."

We both knew that wasn't true. David could do whatever he wanted, and all of Bethel Pentecostal would go along with it, if it meant doing what they thought was right in the eyes of the Lord.

"I think we should probably start to be a little more realistic, don't you?" she asked, trying to make some sort of halfhearted joke.

"We have each other's backs," I whispered, echoing more words from the day of Charity's deliverance. "We're okay as long as we have each other."

She sighed again, curling up against me. I didn't shy away from her touch this time, allowing myself to embrace the warmth of her skin, to be truly, genuinely connected.

"You can't protect me anymore, Abigail." Her voice wavered as she whispered, "I've gotta do this one on my own, and I'm not letting you come with me."

There wasn't much more to say after that, so I let her stay. I let her lay in my blankets, and I wrapped my body around her, doing as much as I possibly could to feel safe. To let *her* feel safe. If you'd asked her, she would have told you that she hardly ever cried, but I know she was crying that night. Even if I couldn't see it, even if she wouldn't admit it, I could feel the gentle shaking of her body and the soft hiccups in her breathing. After a while, it stopped, and Nora fell asleep in my arms.

She slept well that night, sneaking out through my window before the first light of dawn. Drifting in and out of consciousness myself, I watched her sleep. I memorized the lines in her face, the smattering of freckles across her nose. I spent a solid hour just staring at the curve of her hair on my pillow, wishing that this could be my eternity.

If she was right, I wanted to make sure I would remember every single detail of her, forever.

And she was.

That night would be the last time I would get to do anything like that, or even see her so close.

*

I only ever had one conversation with Nora's mother. It was a few days before our graduation, one of the rare times Mrs. Willett and I had ever been together alone. Helen Willett was a decent woman, and she put up with a lot, but I'm not convinced she actually loved her daughter. They looked pretty much the same—high cheekbones, deep green eyes, and chestnut hair. They were both sharp. Taking after her mother was only natural for Nora, I assumed. Mostly because her father was never around, but also because Helen wanted so badly for Nora to be just like her in every aspect. But where Nora questioned, where Nora grew angry and sought to understand, Helen was entirely passive, never wanting to understand more than Bethel Pentecostal and the Lord.

It infuriated Nora to no end.

That day, the question of Nora's fate was looming over all of us.

Typically, after graduation, the girls of Bethel are quick to get married, as I've explained to you. If that isn't an option, they take an easy position, mostly to pass the time until marriage becomes a more viable option. These things usually take the form of jobs like seamstress, teacher, or otherwise. Every so often you'd see a woman become a farmer, but if that happened, you'd be talked about until the end of time, or until you abandoned your position. Often both.

I wasn't set to be married, but I was lucky in the way that my mother was a seamstress, so I didn't need to worry. I could work and take my time with things (and decide whether or not I even wanted to *get* married to any of the boys in Bethel, but that was a reckoning for a later time.)

Nora was not quite so lucky. She had no prospects, and no one wanted her for a job. She hadn't proven herself to be of use in any way and didn't demonstrate any skills that would suit the positions we had in town. I wasn't worried about her, but everyone else seemed to be. Especially her mother.

Growing exhausted by the constant barrage of *What are you going to do after you graduate?*, Nora had vanished for the day, long before I had sought her out. She wasn't by the lake, she wasn't in the forest, so I went to her home. On a normal afternoon, there might've been arguing, or the clattering of pots and pans to indicate that someone had begun to cook dinner. On that day, there was nothing but silence.

Mrs. Willett sat in the living room, head in her hands. She jumped when I entered, looking up with a hopeful sort of expression, which only fell when she realized it was me and not her daughter.

"You don't know where she is, do you?" she asked me.

I shook my head. "I was coming here to ask you the same thing."

She laughed, and an uneasy silence fell between us. I didn't normally make it a habit to talk to Mrs. Willett, considering how much Nora talked about hating her, and how much she had judged me at first for wanting to be Nora's friend. She wasn't particularly close to my mother and didn't really stray outside of her home and her Bible other than for church. I just . . . didn't have a reason to. And she didn't really have a reason to talk to me, other than I was Nora's friend. But even then, Nora wasn't a daughter she was proud of, so how much worth could I possibly be to her?

So when she finally spoke, it was unexpected.

"I'm worried I'm raising a demon, Abigail." I was shocked by her honesty and didn't know how to respond. It felt somehow wrong, that the mother of my dearest friend would come to me with her parenting concerns. Especially considering exactly how close we weren't.

"I wouldn't call her a demon, ma'am. She's a bit funny, sure, but not malicious." There was a balance between reassuring Mrs. Willett and defending my friend, and I was doing my best for both ends.

"I just don't think she's going to thrive here is all."

I worried about what that meant. Thrive *here*. In Bethel. Did Mrs. Willett intend to send Nora away? Would Nora end up like Betsey Allen, or any of the other folks we weren't really supposed to talk about?

And if that happened, what would become of me? Nora was my only friend. She was everything. Not to be dramatic, but I didn't think I could live without her.

"What do you mean?" I asked, hesitant.

"Well, I just think that maybe Bethel isn't the place for a girl like her." Mrs. Willett sat up, taking a sip from the cup of coffee that sat next to her, which I'm sure had long since grown cold. "I've been wondering if this all would be easier if I just sent her away."

There it was. The admission, and the solidification of all my fears. She was going to send Nora away.

I have always been very good at remaining calm in a situation that would normally elicit panic. Maybe it has something to do with the fact that I hesitate so damn much, or I can never truly make up my mind. But in that moment, I couldn't come across as hesitant, or even afraid. I had to be intentional and rational, driven by the pure desire to keep my friend grounded in Bethel.

"You're a good girl, Abigail. I admire the way you've stuck by my daughter after all this time." She sighed. "I just don't know what to do anymore. I'm worried about her."

"I don't know if you're asking my opinion, ma'am," I said, looking at Mrs. Willett, trying to summon any ounce of authority or responsibility or whatever it was that she needed to hear from me in that moment, "but I don't think you should."

"She's just so unhappy," Mrs. Willett continued. "I think she might be better served somewhere else. We have family out in the Dakotas, I could—"

"No!" My heart filled with fear. The Dakotas were far—too far. I would never see her again. Mrs. Willett stared at me, shocked by my outburst.

"I just—" I floundered for something to say. "I think that God wouldn't have brought you to Bethel if he didn't intend for Nora to have a future here."

She seemed to believe me, even if I didn't believe myself. Mrs. Willet nodded to herself, in the same way that I had seen Nora do so many times. They might not have had much in common, but she was clearly her mother's daughter.

"I think," I continued, "that it would be a disservice to send her away, when she's already got so much promise here. And besides,"—I shifted my demeanor, trying to turn this conversation into something more lighthearted—"she has me to protect her, anyway. I'm not going anywhere, and I'll make sure she doesn't get into any trouble."

I think about that conversation now and it never ceases to make me laugh. It made Mrs. Willett laugh at the time, but for entirely different reasons. She thought I was naïve, but sweet, and she was willing to let me keep trying for her daughter.

I wonder now what might've happened if I had let Nora go. If she had been sent to the Dakotas, or to Kentucky like Betsey Allen. Would any of this have happened? Probably not, right? We'd probably still be trapped in that same circle, Elijah and Caleb and Rebecca would be alive, but none of us would be happy. Not even her, I think.

Maybe she could have pretended, for a while. Maybe she could have waited just long enough, and then run away to some big city, finding out what it means to be truly happy.

Or maybe we would have all died alone, and Bethel would have continued on like it was always meant to, holding up the words of the people over the word of the Lord. It's hard to say.

My personal preference is to assume inevitability. I like to think that even if I hadn't said no to Mrs.

Willett, Nora would have found some way to stay, and things would have panned out exactly as they had. To assume that Nora would have done what Nora would have done, and there's nothing I could have done to keep her around any longer than she was meant to be.

Nora reappeared after about an hour, not talking about where she'd gone and refusing to speak to her mother at all. We went about our day, walking around town, sitting by the lake, all of the normal things we did each day. As much as I didn't realize it then, in retrospect, all of it felt like a goodbye.

I never spoke to Mrs. Willett again after that. She wouldn't meet my eyes after everything that happened.

I still see her around sometimes. At church, praying for Nora's lost soul. Wandering the streets, with not much else to do. I don't really pity her, but I'm sure someone else does. I'm sure there are people who comfort her, apologizing for what happened to her daughter and telling her that it was all even in the eyes of the Lord.

I'll tell you what happened and let you decide just how even everything ended up.

VII

I don't think Pastor David was ever truly satisfied after what happened with Caleb. He was mad after Elijah, sure, which is why we had the deliverance. But there was no second deliverance. There wasn't much more he could do, and to go from having two brothers to hold you up to having absolutely nothing except for the walls around you? That's rough. I think he should have pulled his shit together and relied on the church like he always tells us to do, but that's just me.

No, Pastor David was an angry man. And he took it upon himself to convince the parish that Nora just . . . wasn't quite saved yet.

They pulled her out of her home early the next morning, not even an hour after she had left my room.

It wasn't pretty. It was the most upset I had seen Nora the entire time—kicking and screaming and saying all manner of unholy things.

All of Bethel followed them, even her mother, who stood a respectful distance away.

I'm not sure when they decided that it would be the best decision to burn Nora Willett at the stake, or who even decided it in the first place, but if I knew, I promise you they wouldn't be here with us anymore.

Her mother must've signed off on it.

They looked far too calm as Pastor David tied Nora to the pyre, something he must've spent hours building the night before.

As I watched, I wondered what had happened to her successful deliverance. I wondered how far one person had to go to be considered past the reach of God's grace. And I wondered who, exactly, had the authority to determine such a thing.

Nora was screaming right up until the ropes were fastened, and she realized there was nothing more she could do.

The crowd formed around the pyre, thick with every life Nora had ever touched. Leah Parker was there, holding hands with Tommy McClain in a way that made me want to vomit. Ruth Winsby was there, tears streaming down her cheeks in remembrance of her daughter. My own mother was there, silently keeping watch as everyone gathered. Even Nora's mother was present, standing a respectful distance away and looking as austere as she could possibly muster. Her father was absent, of course, and I wondered how he would've felt had he known that David was acting in his place—making suggestions and choices revolving around Nora's existence without his consent or consultation.

Would he have saved his daughter, or preferred to let the Lord do the saving?

It's too late to think about those things now, though, isn't it?

"Nora Willett," Pastor David spoke, mainly addressing the crowd, though his words were meant for Nora. "You have been given your chance. You have been spoken to, you have been prayed over, and we have even attempted to deliver you." He sighed, heavy and deep. Energy and tension filled the air as the people murmured and hummed. "It has been made clear that you are not going to be saved now, nor do you have any plans of listening and learning in the future. Thus, your life will be taken as payment for the lives of Rebecca Winsby, Elijah Taylor, and Caleb Taylor. Do you have anything to say for yourself?"

Everyone shifted to look at Nora, who hadn't been paying attention.

I took a moment, similar to the one from the night before, to memorize everything I possibly could about her. Her dress was white linen, and it flowed in the breeze.

They had built a platform under her feet, so that she could at least stand on the pyre instead of having to hang there.

Her hands were bound with cotton rope, which would surely burn faster than any other part of her would.

Maybe she could get away.

Maybe she could—

Nora spat, and the wind carried it away from her and directly into the face of Pastor David. I had to stifle a laugh.

"Well, if that's all, then." Pastor David sighed again, turning and pulling a small matchbox out of his front pocket.

They burned her as the sun rose, and Nora was the one who started it.

Like everything else about her, it wasn't quite so simple as that. I wish I could say that she struck the match against herself, or Pastor David handed it right over and she—ever the brave one—lit it on her own to prove a point. I couldn't even give you any evidence that Nora was the one who lit it, but I just know in my soul that's the case.

You'll have to take my word for it.

Pastor David didn't say anything as he held out the match. We all knew what was coming. We all knew what he thought and what had been whispered.

He meant to strike it on the book I'm sure, after a moment of tense staring and adrenaline building in all of our hearts. He was mocking her, in a way. Playing with his power and trying to make her feel bad for what she had done.

Before he could, though—before Pastor David could be the one to end Nora's life and take all of the responsibility on himself—Nora looked at me and winked.

At the same moment her eye shut, the match flickered to life, the flame dancing in the wind with the slightest twinkle to it.

Panicked, David dropped the wooden stick into the pyre, and it caught quickly.

Nora was always so determined to be the master of her own fate, it was only appropriate that she started the fire that ended her as well.

I'll do you the favor of not describing the burning in depth. You don't need to know all of that. All you need to know is that Nora was completely silent, not uttering a single sound as the flames licked up her legs and covered her body. The crowd was a dull roar of prayer, people begging for everything from Nora's salvation to their own, as if they knew that what they were taking part in was unholy.

A lot of people think she died silent, and her last words were the indecipherable ones she had screamed as they tied her up, but that isn't necessarily true. She whispered something else, something meant only for me, right before I turned and walked away from her for the last time.

I caught her eye, even though I had been trying not to. I couldn't help myself. The fire illuminated her face in such a perfect way, I had to look.

At that moment, she smiled at me. It wasn't a terrible grin like she had so many times before. It was somber. It was sweet. It felt real.

"I love you," she whispered, and somehow, over the crackling of flame and the murmur of the crowd, I heard her.

She had said a lot of things up till then that I didn't necessarily believe. She had lied about being saved, lied about the direction God was taking her. Kept so many secrets from so many people.

But what she said to me?

I know that was real.

I wouldn't doubt her for a second.

I had to leave after that. It was all too much, and I know she understood. I might know more if I had stayed, if I had watched till the end like Pastor David or her mother, but I doubt they'd be willing to answer any questions. They'd just tell you she's with God now. Or somewhere else entirely. But I couldn't stay to watch the fire die down.

I did go back, though, eventually. Well, a few hours later. When I do my most illicit things—after God and everyone had gone to sleep. Nothing could stop that awful gnawing in my chest that something just wasn't right about the whole thing. And it didn't help that her words kept replaying over and over in my head.

The silence of the crowd, the wash of the flames. Nora's eyes on me—not pleading, not sad. Satisfied. Like she had long been ready for this sort of thing and had just been waiting for someone to finally light the flame. Her mouth forming those words that I knew I would never forget.

I searched for her body, and God-damn me, I looked for a while. I wanted to see if there was anything I could do to give her peace in the beyond, give her something to take with her, or even just say my own personal goodbyes.

It was gone.

You hear that, and I know you're thinking that maybe they just took it away early to prevent something like exactly what I was doing, but no. It wasn't like that.

There was no evidence that she had ever been in the fire to begin with.

Some of her should have stuck, right? Pieces of charred clothes; I would have even settled for chunks of flesh or hair stuck to the wood and ground. A skeleton could have been removed, sure, but every trace of her?

No.

That was when things changed for me.

Something in the way the wind blew, the subtlest shift in the direction of the breeze, had me looking toward the forest.

I don't believe in ghosts. The Bible is pretty clear about the idea of spirits staying behind to haunt the living, and it's also pretty clear that anything I might've thought was a ghost was, at best, a trick of the wind or, at worst, some sort of fallen angel trying in vain to deceive me.

But just at the edge of the tree line, right near where we had found the snake all those years ago, right where she had told me once that she'd run away and hide if she ever got the chance, there was Nora.

She wasn't doing anything there, just standing. Watching me. Waiting.

"Nora?" I called out to her, stepping in that direction.

She didn't move. I ran forward, trying to get a better glimpse of the person in the trees.

Closer and closer I got, but she never became any clearer.

By the time I reached the tree line, when I got to exactly where she should have been standing and waiting, there was nothing there.

I don't try to fool myself into thinking that it was her, or that she would have asked me to go with her in some sort of twisted runaway fantasy, but it sure would have been nice to be able to say goodbye for real.

*

I haven't said this to you yet, and it's the last thing I'll say on the whole matter probably, but part of me believes that Nora always knew this was going to happen. There are a few things that led me to this conclusion, but one of the most prominent ones was a conversation we had when we were about fourteen years old. I'll do my best to recount the events for you below, but you're gonna need to just trust me when I say that when things came to Nora, I didn't try to question her choices too much. I didn't ask her much about what she did or didn't know, or what she thought was or wasn't coming in the future.

I like to think that it was fate that drew us together, putting her on that beach the day after my father's funeral. But if that was fate, then fate was what controlled everything else as well.

A long, long time ago, God gave us the freedom to make our own choices. But I do believe some of us are trapped making the same choices over and over again simply because it doesn't seem like there's any other option. And that can be a kind of fate, too, don't you think? I think Nora felt trapped more than anything else. I think she maybe made a bad choice or two because she felt like she had to, and then all of a sudden she was a bad person, and bad people get bad consequences, whether they actually deserve them or not.

We were by the lake when she told me she knew how she was going to die.

Not by the lake like we were for the kiss, or when we met, but farther down, closer to the edge of the forest. It's funny to think about now, but we might've been in the exact same place where they set up the pyre.

I guess that helps my point that she always knew.

We weren't doing anything important, just sitting and talking about nothing—about school, about how annoyed we were that we had to go to church, about anything, when out of the blue, she asked me:

"Do you know how you're gonna die, Abby-girl?"

I didn't know how to respond. How could anyone respond to a question like that? I had thought about it more often than an average fourteen-year-old, I'm sure. When so much of your life is spent in fear of going to hell, you tend to ponder on those things more than you should. But I'd never tried to nail down the exact how.

"Can't say I do, why?" I responded.

She shook her head. "I'm just thinking about it, you know?"

"Do *you* know how you're gonna die?" I asked her.

"I think so, yeah." She patted the ground with her foot. "I think it'll be fiery, and probably very impressive." She hopped from foot to foot, like she was doing some sort of dance. "Maybe I'll commit a crime, and they'll burn me alive!" On those last words, she turned toward me, lunging out like she was going to attack.

I yelped, pulling away from her. I didn't like the idea that she was essentially describing going to hell, but I wasn't going to mention that. Nora didn't really like it when I mentioned the idea of going to hell.

"That sounds scary," was my response.

"I might run away before then, though," she said.

My young heart seized at the idea of losing my friend, and I shook my head.

"You can't leave me, that's not fair."

She laughed in response to my worry, which caused my face to get hot and contort in an embarrassing way.

"I'm not gonna leave you, stupid!" She bumped her shoulder against mine. "I could never leave you."

We sat in silence for a moment, doing nothing other than listening to the birds and the rush of lake water against the shore. It was a nice day. The weather hadn't been too good recently, but the sun had come out for a couple of moments, which is why we'd decided to spend the day outdoors instead of annoying our parents anywhere else. I wish I remembered more about it. I wish I remembered the way my bravery felt as I took Nora's hand and forced her to look me directly in the eyes.

"You swear you'll take me with you?" I asked, as grave as I could possibly be. "You promise on your life, the way we promised about the snake?"

She looked at me, a profound sense of sadness in her eyes.

Maybe she knew her next words would be a lie.

"I promise you, Abby-girl," she whispered, squeezing my hand. "We don't go anywhere without each other. There's no me without you."

"There's no me without you," I echoed back, because it felt truer than the version she had said.

I sighed, relieved.
Nora couldn't leave me.
She would never.

VIII

I won't tell you anything else now. Not about her. I respect that some people might want to find her, and that's all well and good, but I don't think anyone ever will. There's not a body to be found, and there's not a Nora anywhere nearby that might point you in the right direction. If she even would. She's just gone, or she's dead, or she was taken away by the devil and exists in purgatory for all of her many, many sins. I don't know.

You know everything that I know, and I'm the one who knows the most in this town. If you want to know what it looks like, in my opinion, Pastor David had Nora killed as revenge for Elijah and Caleb's deaths. But that's just the way I see it.

I do regret the last time I saw Nora Willett. I know lots of people don't. Lots of people around here think that Nora's gonna come crawling back, pulling herself with her nails out of the forest, threatening all of us and cursing our land like some sort of heathen witch. It's what she deserved, they all claim. You've talked to them, too, haven't you? They must've pointed you my direction.

They all claim some sense of righteous justice, because Nora was possessed, right? She did have the devil in her—again, if that's what you want to think— so she got what she deserved after her deliverance went all wrong. She deserved what they did to her next.

I don't think anyone deserves that. And I think that if Nora did want to come back—assuming she isn't dead, of course—then they'd get what was fucking coming to them. Pardon my language.

I think a lot about what my mother said, what I told you at the beginning of all of this. Bethel is touched by angels. We're protected here, supposedly, by God and by the people of the community. But no one ever protected her. I don't hardly think you're here to protect her either, or to protect her memory, like some people have claimed. I think you're here to right a wrong, but not really the wrong you should be righting.

No one can hurt her now, and we're all better for it. She doesn't need our protection, because where she is?

She can figure it out, I think.

It's easier to remember her in the moments I've told you about than it is to wonder where she might've gone, or if her soul rests easily. I think of her alive, vibrant and angry, and I prefer to keep that version of Nora in my head, no matter what anyone else says.

I don't know if I'll ever leave Bethel now, even though that's probably what she'd want from me. I can't remove myself from the memory of her because she might just vanish altogether, and then all that would be left of her are the rumors that Ruth Winsby can't keep herself from starting. Someone needs to stay here, to remind them of what they did, and to remind them that Nora was real, she was here, and she was more than just a girl who was considered a little troubled by her community.

Her absence is felt.

Time without her is unusual, and leaves me feeling incomplete, like a broken-open egg. It wasn't that she made me whole, or that I'm incapable of living without her . . . I would have just preferred to live with her at my side. Some days, the emptiness takes over, and my heart spills out of my chest in a way I can't explain.

I go to the lake on those days and pretend I can still see impressions of her in the sand. I let the grains press under my nails and I cry.

I go to the church, seeking out the old bloodstain from Caleb Taylor's death. When I find it, I trace it with my finger and whisper *There's a snake speaking to me, Nora-girl.*

I go to the pyre and pretend that the grass is growing back as it should, that it isn't still charred and broken all these months later, well after it should have been green and thriving again.

I look to the forest, and wonder if her ghost is out there, waiting for me to join her.

Those days won't ever leave me, I know that much. They won't fade like the memory of my father, and Nora won't be so quick to weasel her way out of my heart and my thoughts.

There is a universe where Nora and I are happy. I know this to be true. There is a life where she didn't vanish. I don't know what comes next for me, but I know that. And I keep that in a sweet little jar in the back of my mind, right next to the feeling of her lips on my own, and I take it out when I need it most.

Acknowledgements

I wrote this story much faster than I anticipated, but I think that's because this story has been sitting inside of my mind and heart for much longer than anything else, and once I realized that, there was no question. This book—much like Nora herself—came as a complete shock to me, but the moment I sat down and started writing, I knew that it was exactly what I was supposed to be doing.

Of course, there are a number of people without whom this story would not have been possible, so I will take a moment to thank them, as is deserved.

To Riley, for respecting my astronaut time and always listening to whatever truly insane bullshit I have to say, every single time. To my mom, for providing me endless resources when I reached out with questions about snakes and weird religious stuff. To my dad, for always pushing me forward and convincing me that yeah, being a writer is a career that I can actually have.

Thank you to my dearest friends, you know who you are, for listening to me scream in group chats and over late night DMs about what's going on in my head. Having you makes my life easier in ways I can't even begin to express.

To Amanda, for reading this story and believing in it and being just as passionate about it as I am. Additionally, to everyone who helped Amanda and myself in bringing this book to life and making it as absurdly beautiful and cool as it is.

And of course, a special thank you and message of encouragement to anyone who feels Nora's story a little too deeply. To anyone who understands exactly what she did, and why she did it. This story was written with you in my heart. Keep going. Keep going.

Dori Lumpkin is a queer writer and storytelling enthusiast from South Alabama. Having come from an extensive theater background as well as working in the film industry for a time, they believe that storytelling, and especially horror storytelling, is fundamental to understanding the human experience and the world around us. Their work has appeared in many publications, including *Susurrus*, *The Deeps*, *Crow & Cross Keys*, and *Demons & Death Drops*, among others. You can find them @whimsyqueen on most social media websites.

CREATURE PUBLISHING was founded on a passion for feminist discourse and horror's potential for social commentary and catharsis. Seeking to address the gender imbalance and lack of diversity traditionally found in the horror genre, Creature is a platform for stories which challenge the status quo. Our definition of feminist horror, broad and inclusive, expands the scope of what horror can be and who can make it.